The Queen & Elves Come Here Anon

Book One
of
The Return of the Tribes

By Alice Taylor

ISBN 978-1-918079-01-2

Print Edition

Books of this series are available for download on
Amazon Kindle or
The Rum Lot Publishing
www.rumlot.com

First Edition
The Rum Lot Publishing
Lowestoft, Suffolk, UK
2025

III

Dedicated to my husband Mike and daughter Alex
and to my dear friend and editor Rebecca,
all of whom put up with me
with minimal complaints.

"Over hill, over dale,
Thorough bush, thorough brier,
Over park, over pale,
Thorough flood, thorough fire,
I do wander everywhere,
Swifter than the moon's sphere;
And I serve the fairy queen,
To dew her orbs upon the green.
The cowslips tall her pensioners be:
In their gold coats spots you see;
Those be rubies, fairy favours,
In those freckles live their savours:
I must go seek some dewdrops here
And hang a pearl in every cowslip's ear.
Farewell, thou lob of spirits; I'll be gone:
Our queen and all our elves come here anon.

– Puck, Midsummer's Night Dream,
Willian Shakespeare

Prologue

1939

Eyes riveted on her scuffed shoes, her lank rusty hair hiding her face, the girl stood in the exact centre of the fussy sitting room, a picture of misery. Mr Bunn was uncomfortable, but what could he do? There was a war on now, and not many people had the extra money for piano lessons. If he lost a client, Flossie would be beside herself.

"I don't want to hear that fekkin' noise, not now, not ever. Do you understand, Bunn?"

Mr Bunn murmured another apology, but Mr Miller was building up a head of steam and would not be mollified. Mr Bunn thought he was drunk, but it was hard to tell.

"Look at her Bunn! She's as plain as an old boot. No one is ever goin' to want to see that mug on a stage singin'. Not even in a pub. Her mother pushes these daft piano lessons because she thinks it'll 'elp her get married or maybe she can teach other stupid children if she can't snag a man. I don't wager anyone will ever fuck this sorry sack of –"

"Mr Miller!" Mr Bunn stood up and leaned on his cane. His hand shook. This was too much. Too, too much, even for him.

Miller realised that he had gone too far.

"No singing lessons. I won't stand for it." he snapped. "If you want to keep your job, stick to the piano. For that matter, she can bloody well go to your house from now on so I don't have to put up with it. Her screamin' does my head in and everyone moans about it."

"Yes sir. I understand. I think having her come to my house is far better."

"Damn right. Let her do the walking if she wants the lessons. Right, Caddy?"

Caddy nodded, but didn't look up. She knew better than to meet her father's eyes when he was like this, and "like this" was almost every day now.

Mr Bunn's heart broke for the poor girl, but he collected his five shillings and arranged for Caddy to come to him for her next lesson.

That night, when he told Flossie about what happened, they both agreed that Miller was the most horrible of men and while Flossie preferred students taught in their own houses and not in hers, she didn't see any alternative. Miller was surely making black market money, but however he earned his penny, he had plenty of them, and clients who paid on time were not to be sneezed at.

Next Wednesday arrived, and Caddy took an hour of piano, which is what her parents paid for. And an hour of music theory, violin, and voice which Bunn gave her at no charge. It was, he told Flossie, his little revenge for Miller being such an arse.

Caddy never breathed a word about the extra lessons. Keeping her music to herself was a part of surviving.

Ellen

Ellen dreaded Tuesday, but here it was, and there she was, walking up and down the busy street, searching for 169 London Road South, where she would find The Rum Lot, Purveyors of Baubles and Bits, www.rumlot.com . She knew exactly where it was; she had been there many times before. She had printed off the photo from Google Maps.

Dr Crowe had his phone out and was following his GPS. They all walked right past it.

Three times.

Finally, Mr Assam, Director of the Department of Social Services for the Council and Ellen's direct boss, turned back and pointed, and all three turned on their heels and walked directly towards the shop. Halfway across the narrow street Dr Crowe glanced at his phone; Ellen looked at her watch; Assam looked longingly at the coffee shop. And then it was behind them. Again.

Dr Crowe mumbled to himself and impatiently shook his phone. Impossible. Mr Assam, the one who insisted that they both go with Ellen today, made a choking noise that was halfway between a whistle and a gurgle.

Ellen looked over her shoulder, avoiding their eyes, and hugged her binder close to her ample chest. "Gentlemen, the only way we can get in is to concentrate and stare at the door. Walk right up, and don't look away. All three of us. Otherwise we'll be doing this all day."

"Impossible. This is ridiculous. Doors just don't *move*."

"Well this one does, and it's done that for as long as I've been coming here. I told you this in the office. That's why I come alone. Ten years I've been doing a health and welfare assessment. Every year I come here, check that she is still alive, and go back to write my report. If someone comes with me it takes all day because they never do what I say and then – well – they don't come a second time.

She sighed, not even bothering to hide her irritation, "Now it's you two. Do as I say, and let's just get this over with."

Crowe scowled and looked over to Assam.

"D'you still want to see her?" Assam nodded slowly. Then shook his head. Then nodded.

"Okay." Ellen turned to The Rum Lot's front door. "Look at the open sign; don't look at anything else. Follow me."

They made it to the door and squeezed in the little alcove. Assam could see the interior of the shop through the glass. It twinkled.

Ellen leaned against the shop door hard and gave it a good push. Nothing happened. Whenever she had someone with her the old door seemed to get heavier and stickier. Dr Crowe jumped forward to help, and together they pushed hard against the thick glass. On the other side an old faded sign teased "Open!" but the door obviously had other ideas.

Then, without warning, the door gave way, and Ellen and Crowe tumbled into the dark shop. The bell rang bizarrely loud as the door swung open, as it always did, and, as she always did, Ellen jumped at the noise.

This year she didn't let the door swing back and hit her colleague in the face. Lessons learnt. It wasn't the dignified entrance she was hoping for in front of Dr Crowe and Mr Assam, but they were in.

Their eyes adjusted.

The shop was stuffed – just stuffed – to the rafters with trinkets and baubles, each one a gaudy, glittery delight. Assam and Crowe shuffled in behind Ellen, their eyes as wide as dinner plates as they took in the shiny, colourful clutter dangling from every surface. The walls were painted a dark navy blue, contrasting against the baubles and making some seem to float off the walls. There were Christmas trees, lights twinkling, and old wood dressers that gleamed of decades of polish. From hidden speakers the Andews Sisters sang "Tuxedo Junction". It smelled lovely.

Assam sneezed.

In the very back of the shop was a long, low, intricately carved counter topped with a modern till to ring up sales and tissue paper to wrap the baubles. Sitting behind the counter, tapping on a laptop, was the lady they came to see, Mrs Cadence Aeldor, shop owner and, from their records, a centenarian plus.

She smiled and closed her laptop, but she didn't get up.

"Hello! Ellen, it's so nice to see you again!" She looked at Dr Crowe and Mr Assam, and her smile got a bit broader. Her green eyes glittered.

"Hiya, Ms Caddy. It's lovely to see you, too. You're looking well!" And indeed, for someone as old as Ms Caddy was, she looked quite good. She was neatly dressed in a sensible jumper and dark jeans, her snow white hair was very, very thin and floated around her head, but what she had was combed and neatly held in place by a black Alice band. Her face was a soft mass of fine wrinkles and buried deep in them her bright green eyes twinkled, just like the baubles in her shop. Ms Caddy was of average height and a bit stocky. No one looked twice at her when she walked down the street and that was the way she liked it. She was an absolutely average, middle-class little old lady, and that was her cloak of invisibility.

Caddy smiled at Ellen. She liked Ellen a lot, but it was funny that after one reached a certain age it was always a surprise to younger people that you were still vertical.

"But I'm sure you can guess, Ms Caddy, that I'm not here to buy a bauble today. This is my yearly health and welfare visit. You didn't answer my letters and emails to book a visit, so we just popped in anyway."

Caddy had the grace to look a bit sheepish. She was being a bother for Ellen, and she knew it.

Ellen introduced Dr Crowe and Mr Assam.

Dr Crowe looked at the old woman closely as she sat there. He was there to assess her physical and mental health. She didn't seem to be confused, and she didn't seem to be particularly frail for her great age, but it was early days yet. He typed a "first impressions" note into his phone.

"Mrs Eeldoor –," Assam began.

"It's pronounced ALE-dor not EEL-door."

"I'm so sorry." Assam sneezed again. His eyes were watering.

"It's Old English. It's my married name. It means leader or eternity depending on the context. I think it would be a good name for a pub. What do you think?"

"Yes, madam. May I call you Caddy?"

"No. Mrs Aeldor will do."

Ellen let out an audible sigh. Caddy shot her a glance and decided to be good. The more she cooperated the quicker they would leave.

Dr Crowe tapped another note into his phone.

Assam started again. He was getting cross and was having trouble breathing.

"Mrs Aeldor, my department received a call on our tip line about you. The person was quite concerned that at your extreme age you –," and he hesitated because this was delicate. He didn't want to get into any age discrimination issues and he was talking in front of two witnesses. "__ might be in need of assistance."

The old woman's eyes narrowed. The three visitors were too busy with their own work to notice their angry green flicker.

Someone had called an adult social care hotline about her. And she had a good idea who.

"I'm good, Mr Assam. Just peachy keen. When I want assistance I know who to ask. If you don't want to buy a bauble I think we are done here. Good day."

Now Mr Assam was really irritated. He could barely breathe in here; the damn shop was an assault on his senses in every way, and now this old bat was dismissing him like he was a sixth former in the head teacher's office, and he hadn't even had a chance to tell her what they could do.

"Mrs Aeldor, there are many services that we can offer you. You are, according to our records, over one hundred years old and that in itself gives you first choice in any of our fine facilities. You won't have to pay! From our records, you don't have any relatives, so payment can come from your esta –"

"We are done, sir. Leave my shop. *Now*!" The old woman was furious. Absolutely beside herself. Her face flamed into blotchy red and white and her green eyes snapped. The effect was, Crowe thought to himself, rather Christmasy.

When Assam didn't move, she bounced out of her chair and popped around to the other side of the counter and stood nose to nose with Assam and put her hands on her hips.

"I am NOT going anywhere. I know exactly who called that report in. It was my landlord. She's been trying for the last year to force me out of this lease because she thinks she can get more money out of the place with a new tenant. I have an ironclad lease, and she's now decided to play dirty. Well, I'm not leaving my shop. I'm not leaving my house. And you can stick your fine facility up your –"

"Ms Caddy! Please calm down! No one can make you go into a care home." Ellen's voice was calm and soothing. She had been down this route before with elderly clients. You don't *tell* them they should go to a care home, you lead them – gently – and get them to ask. She knew Assam would screw this up.

Dr Crowe wrote more notes.

Caddy glanced at Ellen and then went back to Assam.

"Get out. You're not welcome in my shop." She crossed her arms across her chest and glared.

And suddenly Assam had a full-blown hay fever/ asthma/panic attack, and the entire shop started spinning, and he knew baubles were going to fly off the walls and that if he didn't get out, and get out NOW, he would be stuck in this tinsely, glittery, fairyland hell forever. He backed away from the awful old crone and ran to the door which gave the impression of opening for him, and before he knew what was happening he was outside, gasping and heaving on the pavement, heedless of the staring people walking by.

Crowe saw him take one last look at the shop and then the man ran – literally ran – back to his car, and that was the last they saw of him.

Ellen sighed.

"Well," said Dr Crowe.

"Well," said Ellen.

"Well," said Caddy, and they all turned back to the counter where Caddy resumed her seat and smiled brightly at her remaining visitors.

"Mrs Aeldor, ma'am, I've written some notes, and if I may please ask a few more questions I'll be on my way. I can tell you right now that I don't see any reason to recommend a more custodial relationship with the Council. If you can help me fill in a few gaps I can write a report and put this telephone referral to bed."

Caddy smiled, as sweet as pie, clasped her hands on the counter and nodded. Ask away.

After a few questions about stairs, stability, eating and bathing, and who was managing her finances to make sure she wasn't being taken advantage of in that regard, Dr Crowe went into a series of questions about her mental state. He didn't ask about her medical history; he already had that.

"Are you depressed, or do you have suicidal thoughts?"

"No."

"Are you lonely? Do you miss not having people around?"

Caddy laughed. "I have plenty of people around! That's why I have a shop! It gets me out of the house. I certainly don't do this for the money!"

Crowe nodded and made more notes.

"Do you lose track of time?"

"I'm over a hundred years old. I lost track of time years ago."

Crowe smiled. "I think I'll put that down as a no."

"Do you get visits from relatives?" And he paused. She had no relatives, it was in her records, but if she had visions or hallucinations –

"Nope, all dead and gone. They don't come back to bother me. They wouldn't dare."

"Is there anything you want me to know? Anything at all that is concerning you?"

"No."

He looked at her. She was old, very, very old. She was born in 19-(fucking hell)-25, and that put her well over one hundred and into the realm of super-agers. But with no one to make a fuss like a care home manager looking for a PR hit her age wasn't known to anyone but a few computer databases, and he could tell she liked it that way. She wanted to be left alone and he had to respect that.

She wouldn't be long for this world. As a physician, Crowe had years of experience with old people and she had that frail, rather transparent, faded look the healthier ones got in the last year of life. He very much doubted he would be back next year for a conversation with the redoubtable Mrs Caddy.

He would sign her off as competent and not in need of Adult Social Services. If they moved her against her will to a care home she wouldn't last the month; he'd seen that happen before, too. Let her die on her own terms, in her shop.

Gemma

The solicitor was firm. Mrs Aeldor had an ironclad lease. It might be a lease with some unusual caveats, but as a commercial lease, there wasn't anything Gemma could do to kick her out.

Gemma looked over to Richard in utter disbelief. They had inherited the property from her elderly aunt, and it never occurred to her that they wouldn't be able to do whatever they wanted to with it.

Wanting to save on solicitor's fees, she and Richard had handled evicting the old witch themselves, but that wasn't working. Richard had sent her a letter stating that her lease would not be renewed and to look for another premise. No answer. They sent a notice that her rents would be raised under a new lease. No answer.

They visited in person and offered to pay to move her to another shop. Mrs Aeldor politely declined the offer and said she had no intentions of going anywhere. She didn't say that even if she wanted to, she couldn't because no one was going to do a commercial rental to an over one-hundred-years-old sole trader. They'd never finish out their lease.

Unknown to Richard, Gemma made an anonymous call to the Adult Social Services hotline to see if they would step in and put the old bat in a care home or something. That didn't work.

They then sent a Section 21 eviction notice to the shop, and Aeldor's solicitor answered with a rather snippy reply, in essence telling them to both get stuffed.

Now her solicitor, who she was paying by the hour and who seemed to work very slowly, was sitting here, papers in hand, and saying that they couldn't do anything at all.

"I know this is disappointing, but the lease is quite clear. You can raise the rent to market value every five years and that happened right before your aunt died, so you can't raise it for another four. It's very unusual, but she has the right of renewal for life. Her life.

She is paying her rent on time; she has done nothing to breach the terms of the lease. She is, by all objective measures, a good tenant and so has "security of tenure," and that gives her rights to the space. You can't evict her."

"But that just can't be! What about my rights? I want that space. I have plans for it!"

"I'm sorry, but I don't see how you can evict her. Have you thought of paying for her new space?"

Gemma frowned. They had already offered to pay for a move, but actually paying for new deposits and remodelling a new shop was not in the cards. That would be expensive and they didn't have that kind of cash.

"I'll think of something." And she grabbed her handbag and told Richard to come along; they were done here. They didn't need to pay for more solicitor time.

Caddy

Someone threw a brick through The Rum Lot's main window. Right through the effing window. Right through the new Christmas display, breaking baubles and nicking the nose off an elf.

Caddy couldn't believe it. She had been on London Road South for over thirty years, opening up not long after Ricky died, and back then the Kirkley neighbourhood of Lowestoft was pretty rough, but now it was so much better. She had never, ever had vandalism at her shop. Not a single time.

She was surprised when it happened and a lot surprised about how upset she was over it. That brick felt like an assault on her person, not a brick through plate glass. She was shaken up.

But Caddy had been shaken up many times in her life, and whatever knots were tangling in her stomach, she still had to deal with it, so she took photos, called the police, taped up the hole in the window with cardboard and packing tape to keep the weather out.

Then she called her insurance company, and they told her to go ahead and get a new window ordered, which she did. While she was on the phone with them she remembered she had cameras, and so she had to look for anything recorded for the police. The cameras showed the brick going through the window but not much else. Just a shape in a hoodie, and that was it.

It took all day to deal with. It was the end of November, her busiest time of year, and she had to manage customers who were shocked and concerned and fellow shop owners on the street who were publicly angry that one of their own was vandalised and privately worried their shop
would be next.

"Mrs Caddy! Who would do such a thing? You're an institution! Everybody loves this shop!" The TIQI vintage shop next door was horrified. The Red Rose florist across the street and Over-the-Hook yarn shop checked their cameras, but caught nothing.

If she heard that once she heard it a hundred times in the next few days. It seemed utterly random and sometimes people just did stupid things. But she had her suspicions.

Ricky

Ricky died in 2004. He cycled to Asda like he loved to do, and since Caddy had asked for some ice cream he was in the frozen foods section looking at the selection when he felt an odd twinge and then fell like a rock on Asda's tile floor, dead from a stroke before he hit the ground.

He was seventy-two and had only been retired for two years from his job in Texas and had only moved back to England and to her seaside hometown of Lowestoft for one. And during those two years they hadn't taken a holiday or really done anything at all but hang around and get used to their new retired life, deal with Lizzie, and occasionally visit Caddy's mother who was as mad as a hatter and in a care home. He loved to look at travel web sites, but it wasn't to be. Life, and now death, got in the way.

Caddy was bereft. Oh, she and Ricky had their arguments especially when the romance faded and he treated her like she was his mother, but she had been with him for fifty-three years.

He was only nineteen when they married in 1948, when she was twenty-three. The hole he left in her life would take a long time to heal, but after losing her two boys she knew grief and how holes in your life were like holes in your flesh. They hurt, they heal, they left scars.

A month later her mother died. Unlike the deep Ricky hole, her mother's hole was not so deep, barely a pinprick, to be honest. She'd had dementia for years, and even before that set in she was a difficult person to deal with. Caddy's brothers had moved on, one to America and one to Birmingham, and it didn't occur to either that they should take care of the old girl even though she loved them best. That was the daughter's job. Yes, Mum was in a care home, but that didn't mean Caddy didn't have visits, care plans, doctors, legal issues, and everything else to deal with, and Ricky was no help at all. It wasn't his mum, so it wasn't his problem. So Caddy took on the responsibility for her mother for her last horrible years.

Her brothers never called or came by when Mum was alive. But they did come home for the funeral, and they made sure they had an equal share of the estate.

After Ricky's death it was just Caddy and Lizzy. Her daughter was her only living child and poor Lizzie was getting old, too. In 2004 Lizzy was sixty-two and was the spitting image in both looks and personality of her father. Every time Caddy looked at Lizzy she saw brilliant, quirky, testy, rigid Ricky.

Lizzy was the one who had the idea of a bauble shop, and like all of the side hobbies she started, she worked obsessively on the project for about two months and then abandoned it before much got off the ground. Caddy, though, was intrigued, and after a bit of research she set up a bank account and put in her first order for stock. Why not? It got her out of the house and she didn't have to look at Ricky's empty chair. She had plenty of money to fund an unpaid side hustle and it was something she could do that didn't take finger dexterity or a lot of physical effort. The shop made everyone who walked in happy.

She thought she would have a shop for a couple of years – just long enough to prove it could be done – and then she would move on to something else.

Decades later, long after Lizzie died, she was still running the shop.

And now her shop had a hole in it.

Caddy

Three days after the brick incident, someone drove by the shop at one in the morning and paint balled the front.

A line of yellow splats went across the shop and up to the hand-painted The Rum Lot sign. No one else was paint balled that night or any other night. Just Caddy's shop.

Two incidents meant the vandalism was a trend, and it was obvious that Caddy was being targeted, but by who? An investigator came by and after his interview with the old woman he suggested that Caddy not go out after dark. Maybe take a week or so off and give the police time to do their work.

"Oh, I can't do that! This is my busiest time of year! You can't tell a bauble shop to shut down four weeks before Christmas. People are putting up their trees now!"

"But it's dark early, Mrs Aeldor. It's not safe for you to be alone on your way home."

"It's dark out at four now because it's the end of November. There are lots of people on the street at four, so I'm perfectly safe to go home then. I won't stay open later than that."

But despite her brave words, she was scared. She was years over one hundred, and she knew that one shove by a kid while she was cycling home and the fall off her bike would break a hip. Then she'd be in the hospital for months if she lived at all. She would lose her shop and probably her life if she broke a hip. They would stick her in a care home.

She stopped taking the short way home, through the alley, and stuck to the main, well-lit road.

Then she was spray-painted and like the other incidents, the hooded figure didn't get caught on the security cameras.

She stood on the path, grim faced, and watched Billy scrub the paint off as best he could from the windows, and he promised to come and repaint the wood bits when the weather would allow.

That night someone with a fake account went on TripAdvisor and wrote a scathing review of the shop. Caddy read it with dismay. She had never had a bad review before. Not many people wrote reviews, but those who did were all positive. This person obviously had never been into The Rum Lot and had never bought a bauble from her, so she wrote a very diplomatic reply to the post making it obvious to all who read it that this was a bogus post. She wasn't confrontational, and she put in a request to the website to delete it, although from all reports that would take months. Caddy hoped it wouldn't affect her summer tourist sales.

Now she had another chore to worry about. She didn't have the time to monitor her social media like she should.

The police came by again, and this time they were much more detailed in their investigation. When they found out that Caddy's landlord had recently given her an eviction notice they decided to follow that up.

In the meantime they asked her again to stay at home for a while. Was it worthwhile for an elderly woman to open up a shop in December? No.

Fear turned to anger. It might not be worthwhile to the police for Caddy to open up her shop, but what else did she have to do? She was old. She had no family. Her evenings dragged as it was. Her customers kept her interested in life, and she had hundreds who would come year after year to the shop with their families and buy a special Christmas bauble. If she closed she would be disappointing families from Norwich to Ipswich. She wouldn't do it.

The next morning, very early, she had a stage floodlight delivered to her shop, and she put it up as part of her window display. She gave the young man who installed it a huge tip and a chirpy "Merry Christmas!", but he was happier with the tip.

Caddy opened as usual the next morning and had a busy day. The harassment was now open news, and, if anything, she was busier than usual as indignant customers walked in, upset that their happy shop with its elderly owner was being victimised so horribly, and there were a good number of pity purchases.

Normal closing time came at four, Caddy locked the shop up as usual and, as she always did, rode her bike home. She had a light dinner and then went straight to bed. Usually she played her guitar for an hour or so, but not tonight.

At midnight her alarm sounded, and she got up, dressed in dark clothes (very dramatic, she thought when she saw herself in the mirror), and walked back to the shop. She slipped in and, without turning any lights on, sat down behind the counter and waited.

The Christmas tree lights in the window twinkled, but sitting behind the counter Caddy was hidden in the shadows. She didn't have the music on and the shop was very quiet with only the occasional creak as the old building grumbled to itself as its ancient bones settled.

She sat and watched the front window, her mind wandering. If no one came she would have wasted her time, but she had nothing but time. She had already decided to go home at three and that would give her six hours of sleep. Thank goodness her dog-walking days were over, and she no longer had poor Maggie to take out every morning.

The street was quiet and it was a rare car that drove by. A bobby stopped and rattled the door, but she said nothing, and he returned to his rounds.

A little bauble sat on the counter, a tiny four centimetre globe, and simply to keep herself awake she rolled it across the counter from one hand to another.

Back and forth, back and forth. It wasn't a perfect sphere; it had a tiny cap at the top so a hook could be threaded through and that cap made the little ball roll oddly.

Caddy concentrated on the bauble. Its mirrored surface caught the twinkly lights from the tree and she watched the bauble roll back and forth, back and forth.

The shop was dead silent, and all she could hear was the tiny scrape of the bauble on the wood countertop, and all she could see was the twinkly lights reflected in the mirror surface, a surface she could almost feel. The bauble rolled to her right hand and she gave it a tap – a bit too hard. It rolled off the counter and she cried, "Stop!"

And it did.

It froze in mid-air, a tiny mirrored sphere floating like a planet among the twinkling stars of the Christmas lights.

Caddy was afraid to breathe, afraid to do anything but stare at the floating bauble. If she took her eyes away it would drop. She knew it would. And then it would shatter on the shop floor and that would be a tragedy.

She breathed in – and breathing in pulled the bauble towards her. She willed it closer with some muscle she didn't know she had and it floated a hand's-width nearer. Then it lifted over the counter. She held out her hand – and blinked. And the bauble dropped into her open hand.

Sweat dripped down the side of her face, and in the reflection on the mirrored surface were two green points of light. Caddy hadn't known her eyes were glowing, but their green glow reflected in the glassy surface of the bauble.

Was she going mad? Had her mother's dementia finally set in? Caddy was over one hundred years old and the odds were not good.

The only way to find out was to repeat it. Madness or hallucination would be the verdict if she couldn't levitate the bauble again. But what if she could? What would that mean?

She looked at the bauble. Willed it to move. And nothing happened.

And that was the point where most sane people would just give up and say, "Oh, I was dreaming."

But Caddy wasn't a dreamer; she was a doer. And she knew from her decades of learning and teaching music that success comes with practice. She would try again.

Nothing happened.

She was not concentrating; she was thinking about what would happen, not about making it happen. Caddy had to repeat what she did before to make the thing float.

She controlled her breathing and focused on the bauble. The smooth surface, the Christmas lights reflected in it, the roundness of it. All of that, everything about the bauble, must come to her. She could feel it, its mass, the elements that made up the glass. And when she could feel it, she had something to pull, to grab.

It rolled over to her.

It was only a few inches and it felt like she was moving furniture, but it rolled.

Heaving for air, sweat dripping, Caddy gripped the edge of the counter so hard her knuckles were white.

There was a noise. She looked up, and there was a shadow at the window.

Caddy slammed the switch, the floodlight popped on with a loud crack, and the security cameras suddenly had a good front-lit photo. She had a good look at the mischief maker.

It was Gemma, her landlord.

Why was Caddy not surprised?

Gemma

Gemma argued that it wasn't vandalism if she was damaging her own property. She argued that point with the police officers who arrested her, with the desk officers at the police station, and with the judge who eventually sentenced her. She argued with her solicitor, her husband, and with the article in the *Lowestoft Journal* that featured her mugshot. No one agreed.

Caddy

The very sweet bobby with a shiny blonde knot of hair peeking out from the back of her helmet was quite stern. You must NOT try this again, Mrs Aeldor. No, you stay home and let the professionals handle these things. What if it had been someone really dangerous? Someone on drugs?

Caddy didn't say that her son Conary would come home higher than a kite on some nasty hard stuff and she could handle him, which is probably one reason he left never to return. But she didn't. The bobby was right and she shouldn't have done that. Not at her age.

They drove her home even though it was only blocks away, and they stayed with her until she closed and locked the front door.

The lumpy mattress she and Ricky once shared was waiting for her, and she slept
a dreamless sleep.

Hunger woke Caddy up, and for a minute she didn't know what was wrong with her. She hardly ever felt hungry any more, but today she was starving. And even though she didn't get a full night's sleep, she felt pretty good.

She had a big bowl of oatmeal, and when she made her lunch to eat at the shop she threw in an extra yoghurt pot. It looked yummy.

The shop was rammed all day. It seemed that someone posted that Gemma had been arrested for vandalising The Rum Lot, and once that got on Facebook it was all over town. Half the people who came in made pity purchases and wanted to talk about the vandalism. Caddy received the last shipment of Christmas stock and between serving her customers, putting new stock out, and restocking from the back room, she was running if you can call what a hundred-plus-year-old woman did when she moved as 'running'. More of a waddle-cum-shuffle, really.

At four o'clock it was full dark, raining, and she was ready to go home. She threw a handful of the 4cm baubles in her bag, locked up, and left.

The routine once she got home was always the same. A very early dinner, watch the news, practise her guitar, a bit of internet surfing or suduko, and then on to bed. Tonight, between guitar practice and the internet, she started a new routine – bauble budging.

For an hour Caddy tried to move baubles with her mind. Sometimes it worked, sometimes it didn't. But at the end of the hour she was noticeably better at it. It tired her out though and she gave up the internet and suduko and went straight to bed.

Caddy

Caddy was so busy at the shop she could hardly think. There was a constant stream of customers, and each one required a cheerful greeting, a listen to, shown the perfect bauble (whatever perfect was), and each bauble had to be rung up, wrapped in tissue, and bagged.

In the massive industry of Christmas decorations Caddy didn't sell anything out of the ordinary. At this time of year every shop and garden centre sold baubles, and while hers were of a better quality and she had an extraordinary selection, in order to be successful as a retailer she had to offer something more. She had to give each customer a reason to make the effort to drive down to London Road South and walk into her shop.

Customers thought she sold baubles, but she knew she sold something much more intangible. She sold an experience. She sold magic.

It was the sensory overload when a customer walked into the shop and was surrounded by Christmas magic that sold a bauble, not the price on the tag. Magic meant listening to stories of Christmases past, of smiling the ten thousandth time at "Ohhh! My nan had a bauble just like this!" or finding the perfect shade of blue to decorate a modern showpiece tree. Every customer had their own tastes and their own memories and the reason they came into the shop was to get Caddy's personal service and 'the experience'. Caddy was always mindful that the mass marketers sold much the same thing she did for a lot less money and if the quality wasn't as good in the discount shops that didn't matter to most people.

She didn't make much money with the shop. There wasn't much of a bauble demand in January! But if she managed her money wisely and sold enough Easter and Halloween decs and souvenirs in the summer, the shop ticked over, and it was the eight-week lead up to Christmas when she made any profit at all.

The Rum Lot was never intended to provide a standard pay-the-mortgage feed-the-family living. Caddy didn't need to do that since she had her teacher's pension from her years in Texas, but it was a point of pride that she didn't take money out of the household pot to pay expenses for the shop, and she never did.

When she first opened The Rum Lot Caddy's goal was to make a modest profit and maybe use that money for a holiday. Maybe go on a cruise. But she never went on holidays. Life always seemed to get in the way of holidays and cruises and when Ricky died she just didn't have the heart for it. She and Lizzie would just get on each other's nerves on a holiday, and Lizzie didn't like the idea of cruising anyway. Caddy didn't see any point in going by herself and without making a decision one way or the other holidays just never happened. Her time to roam had passed. Lizzie went on holidays with her husband Joe, Caddy would babysit her dogs, and that was the way it was.

So Caddy stuck any extra Rum Lot money in the bank and when it accumulated she would buy some shares of stock and forget about them. And when Lizzie and Joe were alive she paid for their holidays.

The shop had been open for over twenty years now. People stopped coming in and asking how the hell a bauble shop could survive in Lowestoft and started coming in and telling her they made a point of visiting every year. The Rum Lot had become an institution, an annual trip to celebrate the season and buy one special fun bit of nonsense for the kids.

Then it became a family event to buy a memory for the grandkids. Caddy never had any grandchildren, but she probably entertained more grandchildren in her shop than most places.

Bauble sales peaked the first week in December. Caddy worked totally alone in the shop, and this was the time of year she could really use some help. But taking on a sales clerk was just not practical. During the ten slow months of the year she didn't want to run a deficit by paying someone to stand around, and during the two busy months she didn't want to bother with training and managing someone. Training a new employee was making more work not making less work, and she didn't see the point of it. The shop was small, and two people with not much to do would just trip over each other. She wasn't going to sit at home either. Why? Caddy told her friends she was a shark. If she stopped swimming forward she would suffocate and die, and she wasn't kidding.

She was almost eighty when she opened The Rum Lot, a ridiculous age to start a new business, but that never occurred to her. Caddy never felt her age. She felt her many aches and pains, but she had had physical pain all of her adult life. Her bones creaked and rattled and deformed with arthritis that flared up when she was twenty-seven and pregnant with John, so to her arthritis was not a sign of old age, it was a pain in the ass. In her mind, she wasn't a kid, but she wasn't old either. Inside, she was about thirty-five or forty, and that was how she acted.

Caddy was comfortable with who she was and really rather happy she wasn't a kid any more with all of the insecurities and inexperience youth brought. Age had its ups and downs, but youth was painful all by itself. Caddy's youth was pretty horrible and she wouldn't go back to those times for all the money in the world.

Caddy never met an active, happy old person who wanted to go back to their twenty's, much less their teens. In their own heads they all were about forty – neither young nor old. The ones who wanted to be twenty again were sad and the ones who felt their true age were dying. Everyone else looked in the mirror and surprised themselves at how wrinkled they were because they didn't feel that old inside.

This time of year Caddy felt her calendar age. She rose every morning at six and worked on her website, invoices, and catching up with her books, dreary chores she hated. Then she would shower, make lunch, and go to the shop to gather and box up the mail orders she received the night before. Now, for some reason, she was always hungry and she had to spend extra time making breakfast, too. She started buying protein bars and chewing on them while she worked at the computer which left crumbs on her keyboard, but she didn't see any alternative. She lost weight.

She practised levitating the baubles in the evening. It was tiring, and she really didn't see what practical good it would do her to move a tiny bauble across a table, but she persisted anyway. It was an interesting and certainly unusual talent, and it made her feel a bit giddy. Special.

This new ability to levitate baubles was Caddy's secret, but it wasn't a hard secret to keep. She had no one to talk to anyway. Her close friends had all died off, and she had no more family. No one ever came to her house, and the only people she talked to throughout the day walked through the front door of the shop, and they talked about their own needs. When Dr Crowe asked if she was lonely and she said no she was telling the truth then. She wasn't lonely. But now she was. For the first time since she was in her teens she felt a bit alone.

If you can make magic and you can't share it, what was the point?

Caddy

By the second week in December bauble demand trailed off. Christmas trees were already on proud display and customers now looked for last minute gifts or bought memories for their children and grandchildren.

Life eased back to normal. Caddy always shut the shop for her winter break a few days before Christmas and didn't reopen until mid January. This gave her time to decorate her own house and do last minute shopping for her family.

No tree went up during her girl's last years because she wasn't going to come over to Caddy's house anyway, and after her daughter died, the irony for the bauble shop owner was that Christmas was just another day. Well-meaning friends invited her for dinner, but Caddy couldn't think of anything more appalling than spending Christmas Day as the pitiful, needy neighbour sitting in the corner intruding on other people's family celebrations.

This year, a letter came in the post, and she had other things to think about.

On December 20th a letter from the National Health Service (NHS) was laying on the floor when Caddy opened the front door. It was a fat one. Fat letters from the NHS were never good and this one was no exception. Her yearly poo screen for bowel and stomach cancer was positive and she needed to contact her surgery right away to set up an appointment for further tests.

The letter went on to emphasise that this test result did *not* mean she had bowel cancer but not to delay further investigation. The computer that wrote the letter told her not to worry. Then it thoughtfully added three brochures detailing how terrible bowel cancer was and what to do with a bowel cancer diagnosis. The third brochure was for end-of-life care.

There are moments when time stops. Time had stopped when each of her children died. It had stopped when Ricky died. It stopped when Caddy read that letter.

This was it.

This was what her end was going to be.

Caddy was almost a decade over one hundred years old. There would be no operations or chemo. And if there were, why would she want the last months of her life to be consumed with that horror? She knew people, several people, who had died of bowel cancer. It was curable if caught early, just like Lizzie's breast cancer should have been. But sometimes the doctors opened a person up to take out a tumour and then just closed them back up again. Early was a relative concept.

The morphine never cut out all the pain; she knew that for a fact and Lizzie's slow and painful death was still a raw wound. Caddy could live forever and never forget nursing her daughter through to the end. She'd never forget sitting on the side of her bed that last night, holding her Lizzie's hand, totally alone, and watching the light slowly fade from her baby girl's terrified, hollow eyes.

There would be no one to hold Caddy's hand.

But the odd part was that she felt fine. She had no stomach pains; her gut processed her food just like it always had.

Was the new hunger she was experiencing a symptom? Then there was the tiredness. Caddy was sleeping more and the sleep was not the fitful dozing of old age but a deep and, to her, restorative sleep.

Caddy balled up the letter and threw it in the recycle bin. She missed. Then she slowly went up the stairs to bed and did not sleep well. Not at all.

The next morning she called her surgery and explained about the letter, and she was told to come in that afternoon, the doctor would squeeze her in, and that was certainly not a good sign. She didn't want to be squeezed in. She wanted to be told not to worry, to have a nice Christmas and the doctor would see her next year. But no, she was being squeezed.

Dr Grayson

Dr Grayson took a good look at the ancient woman sitting next to her desk and then looked at the test results on her computer screen. The computer was adamant.

Mrs Aeldor was being eaten alive with stage four bowel cancer. The numbers were all there; the automatic systems at the central lab in Cambridge had screened the poo sample twice. Artificial intelligence analysed the results and there was no doubt. The poor dear was riddled with it.

She hated this. Telling patients there was no hope was not the fun part of being a doctor.

But the old girl looked fine. Grayson saw fifty-year-olds every day who walked slower, had greyer skin, and simply looked sicker than this Mrs Aeldor who was working on her second century. The woman could pass for eighty, maybe even seventy.

She looked at Mrs Aeldor again and then asked a very unscientific,
very old-fashioned question.

"Mrs Aeldor, how are you feeling in yourself?"

Caddy considered this. She knew exactly what the doctor was asking. It was a question people asked back when she was young before sophisticated tests and decades before anything like artificial intelligence was used as a diagnostician. It was a question asked when people had to trust their own knowledge of their own bodies. No one asked that question any more.

"Really, doctor, I feel fine in myself. No problems."

"And no problems with your back passage? No constipation?"

"Nope, everything is working as it should."

The doctor frowned, puzzled, and wondered what she should recommend. This woman was genuinely very old. Even a colonoscopy was a huge risk and exploratory surgery was out of the question. But then what was the point of either? Make her suffer through those operations just to satisfy a doctor's curiosity?

"I'm very sorry to say this, Mrs Aeldor, but the test results are showing stage four bowel cancer. I can't be very optimistic, not at your age."

Caddy nodded. The pleasant expression on her face did not change.

"We can do further tests in preparation for an operation after the New Year, but –"

"No." Caddy cleared her throat. "No, thank you, Dr Grayson." She sighed and
looked at her hands.

"I'm very old, Dr Grayson." Caddy blinked and her eyes had a wet shine to them which made them look very green.

No more needed to be said.

Dr Grayson's voice was soft. "Should I put down that you are refusing
further treatment then?"

"Yes, ma'am. I've thought this through."

Grayson nodded and thought to herself, I'm sure you have. Then in a more matter-of-fact voice she went through Caddy's treatment options, wrote out a prescription for morphine ("when you need it") and said that an end-of-life specialist would contact her, probably after the New Year when they returned to work after the holidays.

"Do you have someone to take you home today, Mrs Aeldor?"

"I'm fine, Dr Grayson. Thank you."

Caddy

It didn't hit Caddy at the shop when she walked from the surgery to pick up her bike and close up for the day.

It didn't hit Caddy when she got home and made her dinner of a kipper and a
few boiled potatoes.

It hit Caddy when she picked up her guitar.

And she started to cry. It wasn't fair. She ate well, she didn't smoke, she hardly drank any booze, she had no family history of cancer. It wasn't fair.

She was feeling good, better than she had for years. The extra guitar practice was even making the crooked little finger straighten out, and she could reach chords she hadn't been able to play for decades.

She could do magic! Okay, it was useless magic, but she could move small light things with her mind. She had kept a feather floating for ten minutes the other night. No one in the world had any use for a magical feather floater, but as a parlour trick it was pretty cool.

It wasn't fair. She went to the kitchen and poured wine in a water glass and took a big drink.

And don't say, Oh, Caddy you've had a good run, you've lived longer than 99.99% of humans. Longer was not long enough. She still had things to do. She still had feathers to float.

She would get the lease stuff with the shop worked out. She had spring catalogues to go through and orders to make. She was making some progress with regaining her old playing skills that life and Ricky made her set aside, and the levitation thing was progressing, too.

She felt good in herself and it wasn't fair.

Caddy didn't want to die like poor Lizzie, emaciated, out of her mind with morphine, dying by inches alone in a dark room with a nurse who kept looking at her watch. Caddy wanted to die like Ricky, upright and doing something he enjoyed until the last minute of his life and then *poof* he was gone. That was the way to go.

She had another glass of wine. There was no reason to be moderate now.

No, if she was going to die, dammit, it would be on her own terms.

I am not. Not. *Not*. Going to die like Lizzie.

If she still lived in Texas she would have taken one of Ricky's guns and finished it off right there.

But this wasn't Texas, it was end-of-the-world Lowestoft, and Caddy lived in a country that severely restricted gun ownership and she didn't have a gun.

She considered her alternatives. The doctor's morphine prescription? No, after nursing Lizzie through her hallucinations Caddy didn't want anything to do with morphine.

Everything else came across as too painful, too slow, or too messy.

Then she heard a seagull cry and she knew what to do. She would walk into the sea. It was December and in December the North Sea was very, very cold. At her age she would die of exposure quickly and that would be the end of it.

That was it. She would walk down to the beach and march into the sea. Suicide by sea water appealed to Caddy's romantic, theatrical side. She looked at her guitar. She would miss her guitar and she was playing so much better now. She started to cry again.

Nope, no time to wait, best get it done.

Grabbing the bottle of wine and her guitar, Caddy walked out the door and didn't look back. She didn't put her coat on; she didn't even bother to lock the door. For the first time in a hundred years she left the house without a hat.

It was almost midnight of the winter solstice, Yule, the longest night of the year. She walked the short block to the Promenade and made her way down the cliff, drinking the wine as she made her clumsy way across the wide sandy beach, staggering a bit. Damn sand kept making her lose her balance.

The sea was wide and wild as the North Sea always was and always would be. It was beautiful, shimmering in the dark and Caddy gloried in the cold wind and the taste of salt in the air. On the Prom the only man-made light came from the lampposts and their weak human glimmer reflected tiny pinpoints in the grey and black water, as inconsequential as the humans who slept in the terrace houses behind her. The winking stars and the fading gibbous moon was the only thing that made the sea visible. The moon turned to her and said it was time to let go of the past and prepare for new beginnings and the stars agreed. Swaying a little, the wind was pretty stiff, Caddy nodded and accepted their judgement. It was time for her to move on and who was she to argue with the universe?

The crashing waves were loud and rhythmic, making their own sea song.

She loved that wild sea song.

The sea deserved songs.

The sea was going to do her a massive favour, so Caddy would give the sea a song before she walked in and gave herself to him.

Was the sea a him?

That felt right.

The sea was a he.
Caddy giggled and drank the last of the wine and threw the bottle into the crashing waves.

Bye-bye bottle!

She would sing a hymn to him. A hymn him. Or a him hymn. Whatever.

Caddy stood on the boundary of two worlds, perfectly balanced. She stood where the finite land met an infinite sea, with her heels on the land and her toes in the cold, cold water.

Caddy strummed her guitar and began to sing. She sang her heart out to the sea. She sang and played and reached deep into her lower octaves because that's what the sea demanded and that's what it deserved. Deep bass notes and throbbing drums, that was sea music.

She could sense vibrations from her song making their own waves and when she felt that, she pushed it, pushed it hard, pushed the vibrations with the same muscle inside her that she used to push those baubles.

Her eyes were beacons of green light and her body glowed with green fire, but she didn't see any of that because she was lost in the song and nothing mattered but singing to the sea.

When the song was done, because songs always end, she waded into the icy sea until the water came to her waist, and with a final echoing cry she threw her guitar into crashing waves and passed out, welcoming the freezing water and enveloping blackness.

A good end to a good life.

Caddy

"*OhMyGod*, Jason, she's alive!"

Caddy's eyes flew open. She was choking. Staring at her, only inches away from her face, were two shocked faces. One had really bad breath. She was choking because one of the shocked faces was trying to ram his fist down her throat to look for dentures or something before he gave her mouth-to-mouth resuscitation.

She batted his hand away and sat up fast, too fast. She head-butted one, lord knows who, and that made her see stars. A dog was licking her toes.

Caddy jumped up and left the two dog walkers kneeling on the sand, mouths agape and staring, and all Caddy could do was go full-on British and back away, apologising profusely for giving them a fright. No, she was fine, thank you very much. So sorry to be a bother. Thank you for trying to save me, but I had just fallen asleep. No, please don't call an ambulance. No worries. So sorry. Ta. Extremely grateful –

And she ran home as fast as her legs would carry her, praying that none of her neighbours saw her. Goodness knows what she looked like. No coat, no shoes, soaked to the skin, and freezing. She wasn't even wearing a hat.

The unlocked front door flew open and slammed behind her, and she ran to the bathroom and turned on the shower full heat and full blast and stepped in, shivering, stinking of seaweed, and covered in sand. She also had a splitting headache. It was all she could do to comb out her skimpy wet hair, make a bun and then crawl into bed, turning the electric blanket up as high as it would go.

Four hours later, Caddy woke up, light-headed with hunger. She made her way to the kitchen and put a frying pan on the hob and broke five eggs into hot butter, and she fried them up, over easy, just the way she liked them. Those eggs were served with sourdough toast and she was in heaven. She ate until she couldn't eat any more.

In the sitting room she found some bananas and she was on her second one when she saw her phone flashing and went to check her messages. There was one from the surgery.

The whole cancer thing was a mistake. The poo machine needed to be recalibrated. Her shit was fine.

Sincere apologies for the mix up, and they hoped she was not too severely inconvenienced.

Caddy

It was December 24th, and The Rum Lot was now officially closed for the season. Only a few chain stores like the Co-Op were open, and they would soon close early. None of the little independents were open, and the normally bustling street was very, very quiet.

Caddy had traded right up to the 24th this year, and the final total was very good. She was pleased with how sales went despite the upset from the vandalism and closing for the doctor's visit. It wasn't a massive lift, but three percent over last year, and that was good enough. She would pay off the extra stock she had bought for the Christmas season and have enough to stock up for Easter, and the shop would muddle on another year.

She puttered around the shop, tidying up, taking out the rubbish so it wouldn't stink up the place when she shut it up for the holiday – that sort of thing. At three she turned off the lights, locked it all up, and rode her bike home in the rain and with the last light of the day fading away.

At her front door she fumbled with her keys, wishing she had turned on the porch light. She thought she had, but she hadn't. She went inside and hung her hat on the hall butler – and froze.

Something was not right.

It all *looked* right, but it wasn't right, and she couldn't put her finger on it.

Cautiously, she sat on the hall bench, took off her boots, and hung up her coat.

There was nothing to see. She peeked in the kitchen and it was empty. Then she carefully looked around the corner to the sitting room and it was empty. There was no place for a burglar to hide anyway.

But it didn't feel right.

Then it hit her. Nothing was out of order. The place was clean. Really clean.

That was it! That's what was wrong. A burglar had broken into her house and hoovered. He or she had hoovered, dusted, and done the dishes.

Nothing was missing; nothing was out of place; it was just a lot cleaner.

Caddy didn't know what to make of this. She carefully took a rolling pin out of the kitchen and walked up stairs, examining every room of the three-story house. No one was there, but it was certainly tidier.

Caddy hated cleaning. She was naturally a rather neat person, but her entire life, as long as she could remember, she tidied up after other people, and she *did not* like it. Starting with mopping the floors after her brothers tramped through with muddy boots, to scrubbing neverending halls in government war offices on her hands and knees when she was a WREN in the Women's Royal Naval Service, to clearing up after Ricky who was an only child and thought that women actually enjoyed housework, she cleaned up after other people and hated every minute of it.

Other women might enjoy a good mop, but Caddy didn't. She despised it, and now that she lived alone she only did what was necessary to keep a reasonably sanitary house. She mostly managed it by not using anything. She used one glass to drink from, one pot to cook in, one bedroom, and one bathroom. Everything else was cleaned by professionals once a year and then shut back up. She used to have a cleaner come in once a week, but the woman had the unmitigated gall to break her arm tripping off a curb. She never came back after that, and Caddy never bothered to hire anyone else.

So her house was tidy at first glance, but there were spider webs in the corners and dust on the surfaces, and if the elderly Caddy couldn't reach it, it didn't get touched until the yearly clean.

Someone had cleaned her house. It was weird. How do you call the police on that?

"Hello, officer, I want to report a drive-by hoovering. No, nothing was stolen. No, there is no evidence of breaking in. It was just that I came home and the dust bunnies in the hall were missing."

Nope, that wouldn't fly, and she didn't bother to call them.

So she shrugged it off and went to make dinner. Maybe someone wanted to give her an anonymous Christmas present. It would have been nice if they left a note or something.

Dinner was tinned ravioli and tinned green beans. Plop plop and into the microwave and done. Then she did her usual evening routine and went to bed.

Morning came as morning always does, and Caddy made her creaky way to the bathroom to pee, shower, and get ready for the day. Standing at the sink she looked in the mirror, which she didn't usually do because it was depressing, and was a bit startled. She didn't look like a witch today. She looked – and she blinked and peered again – a little better, a little brighter. Younger?

She chuckled to herself, "The dementia is setting in. I've lost ten years!"

She unscrewed the cap from the toothpaste and stopped.

She never screwed the cap on her toothpaste. Caddy usually dropped the caps, and they fell behind the radiator. So why was this one on?

Then, brushing her teeth, she looked around. The bathroom was spotless. Towels neatly hung from the rails. No white hairs or dust bunnies on the floor. The shower looked brand new. The sink sparkled.

She showered and was out of there in record time, peeking around corners and holding the rolling pin at ready.

The kitchen was equally spotless. And there was porridge simmering on the hob.

This was getting ridiculous. Caddy felt violated and a little bit scared that someone was coming and going in and out of her house as they damn well pleased *while she slept.*

Caddy looked at the porridge and at the kitchen and back at the porridge again. She made herself a bowl and sat down to think. No point in throwing away good oatmeal.

She considered and rejected the notion that she had a ghost. For one thing, the idea that someone's spirit would cross space and time to break a teacup was always a silly one.

Poltergeists, even benign ones that did the hoovering and made breakfast porridge, were a waste of energy. She had never heard of an obsessive-compulsive house cleaning ghost.

The other issue about ghosts was, if one existed, who would it be? It certainly wouldn't be Ricky or Lizzie. Lizzie was no more a lover of housework than Caddy was. Even worse!

Ricky simply didn't see disorder and dirt. Cleaning was something the fairies did, and if there were no fairies around, then it was whoever was acting as mom. Caddy never, ever forgot the time during an especially fraught period in her life when she was managing three children and a full time teaching job, and she asked him to take out the rubbish in the morning and put the bin out. He was very agreeable and wanted to help out, so in the morning she bagged it up, sat it in the middle of the front door and went back to getting the kids ready for school. All he had to do was take it out and then put the bins on the curb, giving her two extra minutes in her morning.

He stepped right over it. He didn't see it. He stepped over a huge black bag of stinky rubbish, went to his car, and drove off to work. And when he came home he was the most surprised person in the world that Caddy was angry over it.

So any housework obsessive ghost wasn't going to be Ricky.

But just in case, it would be rude not to thank whatever or whoever was cleaning her house, so she did.

"Thank you for cleaning the house. You've done a very good job. It must have been a lot of work."

Silence.

Caddy shrugged. She didn't know what she was expecting by way of an answer. A bill?

The shop was closed over the holidays so Caddy went to the sitting room and wasted the morning surfing on the internet, playing sudoku, and generally messing around doing a lot of nothing.

Then she wandered into the kitchen around lunchtime, and there on the counter was a plate of cold salmon, a bit of salad, and a warm fresh roll. She looked at it for a long minute and then took it back to the sitting room. It would be a pity to waste such a lovely lunch.

"Thank you!"

And that's the way it was for the next two days. As hard as Caddy tried she never saw her invisible housekeeper, but the house remained spotless and meals were prepared. She noticed that he or she even did the laundry and made some minor repairs. It was a full-service ghost.

On Christmas Day, she took a half hour to cycle down to her shop and picked up a bauble. It was a pretty one, deep navy blue with silver and gold stars and a moon on it. She wrapped it in a gift box, put a bow on it and went back home. That night she wrote a card thanking the ghost and asking him (or her?) to have dinner with her on Boxing Day and left it out in the kitchen as a Boxing Day present. There, she thought to herself, let's see what you do with *that!*

When Caddy came down for breakfast on Boxing Day, the kitchen was firmly closed. Her breakfast was on a tray in the sitting room. Caddy could hear muffled noises in the kitchen, and when she went to the door and peeked through the keyhole, someone had stuffed a towel in there so hard it almost came out the other side, so she took that as a hint and didn't try to look again.

She sat by the window with her small Spanish guitar on her lap, wrapped up with an electric blanket, dozing and watching the dreary, rainy day ooze damply by.

At exactly one o'clock a bell rang in the kitchen, making Caddy jump. The kitchen door swung open and she walked in to see her kitchen table set with her best old china, inherited from Ricky's mother. In the place of honour was a platter of a whole roasted bass surrounded by vegetables, along with a basket of bread, bowls of salads, and on the counter was a cake and a trifle. It was a lovely meal without being excessive. It was just right.

"Well, you have really outdone –" The doorbell rang.

Caddy trotted to the door, irritated that someone was calling on her on Boxing Day. Probably trying to sell her a new internet package. She swung open the door, and a child was standing there.

Only it wasn't a child. It was the most shaggy-haired, pathetic, miserable, painfully thin little man she had ever seen. He was cold and shivering, but what would anyone expect if you were out on the rainy street in late December wearing nothing but a short toga? It barely covered his bits.

Caddy stared. He stared back, obviously terrified. She opened her mouth, licked her lips, and frowned. This little man was not selling internet deals, so she invited him in.

"Please come in. Do you need a towel? You're soaking wet."

He sidled in, trying his best to be as far away from her as possible, but the hallway was very narrow so he wasn't too successful.

He shook his head and spoke in a trilling, musical language that Caddy didn't recognise but that teased the corners of her brain. She could almost understand it.

"So no towel. You're okay."

And he shook his head and twittered again. No towel; he was fine.

Caddy took a deep breath. "I assume you are here for dinner."

He looked terrified and miserable. His eyes shot around like a rat in a maze, looking for escape, and then nodded his head as if that was the worst doom he could bring on himself. Guilty as charged, ma'am. Kill me now.

So Caddy smiled her sweetest smile. "Then you are most welcome to my table, sir. Thank you so much for coming." It was a bit stilted and archaic, but the man wore a toga. Her words seemed to fit the situation.

She almost had to shoo him in, but he walked into the kitchen and an unsurprised Caddy noticed he was not surprised by what he saw. He hopped up on a chair, and his eyes never left her face. Considering how grey and skinny he was, he didn't seem interested in the food.

"Well, sir, I suggest we start before this wonderful food gets cold. Please allow me –" and she served him a nice helping of the fish and a bit of each of the side dishes. Then she served herself. His face flushed from red to white and Caddy was sure he was going to stroke out right there and plop face down in the fish, but he recovered. When she took a bite of her fish, he took a bit of his fish. When she used her fork in the American style, he used his fork in the American style. She switched to British, and so did he.

He didn't say a single word, so Caddy thought she'd try a little experiment.

"Could you please pass the salt?"

Oh goodness, she thought he was going to have a fit and fall off his chair. The twisting, the agonies, the faces! But he passed the salt to her as if he was handing vials of ebola to a cobra. She thanked him and used a tiny bit (the fish was perfect as it was) and thought about her next torture.

"What's your name, sir?"

He started, he choked, and then he spat a little trill that Caddy couldn't understand. She tried repeating it, but obviously got it wrong, so he said it again. Again she got it wrong.

"Well, I'm mucking this up." she sighed, "Do you mind if I call you Tony until I get this right? I'll try again later."

Tony nodded. By the end of the evening she had perfected the glottal stop that allowed her to say his name properly and not, as she found out later, the Elvish word for "cheese".

She asked him a few more questions and found that if she didn't overthink it she could understand what he was saying, and so they had a conversation of sorts. He was, she learnt, an elf. He *did* have large pointed ears, but Caddy didn't think she should mention it because that would be rude.

Why did he come to her house? Because she was here.

Why did he clean her house? Because it was dirty.

Why did he cook for her? Because she was hungry.

And it went on like that for a good half hour.

Eventually, he was calmed down enough to choose the chocolate cake over the trifle for pudding, and when that was dutifully eaten, Caddy asked if he wanted to go home now (wherever that was) and he gratefully said yes. As soon as Caddy nodded, he popped away. It was more of a snap than a pop, and with a little flash of golden sparks, he was gone.

"Well!" said a startled Caddy, "And a good night to you, Tony. Sleep well. You made a wonderful meal."

There was no answer, and Caddy went back to finish off the very excellent trifle.

Caddy and Tony

The next morning when Caddy walked in Tony was in the kitchen frying up some eggs. He still looked like a miserable, tortured soul, but Caddy was happy to see him anyway.

"Good morning, Tony!"

He stuttered out a "Good morning, Lord Cadence Miller Aeldor of Lowestoft in the County of Suffolk," and then bowed, only backwards. It gave the impression he was mooning her, and for a brief minute she thought he was taking the micky with her, but no, he was much too terrified of her to joke about anything.

Tony gave her the eggs by positioning himself as far away from her as he could and sliding the plate to her with the tip of his finger as if he were feeding a tiger. A really grumpy tiger. Then he repeated the process with a plate of buttered toast.

"So Tony, last night you said you came to this house because I was here. So I assume you were looking for me?"

He spoke in the musical, twittering language, so Caddy had to ask him to please speak in English because it seemed he knew it. It was easier even though the more he trilled and tweeted the more she understood it.

He nodded. He was sitting as far away from her as he could possibly be, on a stool in the far corner of the kitchen.

"How did you find me?"

"I smelled you, Lord Cadence Aeldor of Lowestoft in the County of Suffolk."

"First, you can call me Ms Caddy, pronounced Miz KAY-dee, because that's what my students used to call me and that's formal enough for me."

"Yes, Ms Caddy, Lord Cadence Aeldor of Lowestoft in the County of Suffolk."

"Just Ms Caddy. That's it. It's shorter and I'm very old. I don't have time for long names." she returned to her questions. "You smelled me! You must have a very good nose! What do I smell like? I take a shower every day."

Tony looked uncomfortable. "This house was very dirty. You've been living here a long time with no elves to clean it, so it wasn't hard to find. The smell was strong. What do you smell like?" He thought for a minute. "You smell like rosemary and mint."

"Well, that's not too bad –"

"With notes of rose and dead civet cat."

"Oh." That wasn't good. "I hope it's not too strong."

"It's much better now. The house is clean."

"I guess it's good a house elf is here now."

Tony was offended. "I am *not* a house elf. Housekeeping is *not* my profession. I'm only doing it out of necessity because no one else is around."

"What is your profession, Tony?"

"I'm a bank manager."

Caddy was startled. "Elves have banks?"

"Of course we do. You can't keep all of your money under your pillow. I managed commercial banking and oversaw an investment division."

"Goodness, that's a long way from making my toast in the morning! What do
other elves do?"

"There are no other elves, Ms Caddy, not any more." And he popped out.

He didn't come back until lunchtime, when his thin, morose face looked even thinner and sadder. Caddy felt sorry for him. She didn't mean to hurt his feelings or dredge up bad memories, but it was obvious that's exactly what she did. There must have been thousands, if not hundreds of thousands of elves like Tony to support a bank with a commercial division, and he said they were all gone. What happened to them?

Caddy and Tony

Caddy sat at the kitchen table, drinking her tea and tapping her spoon on the table. It was a nervous tic that used to drive Ricky crazy, and early in their marriage they had a lot of quarrels over it. Ricky had his fair share of tics, but at least she didn't go into hand-flapping, door-slamming meltdowns when she was stressed. No, Caddy just got quieter, and if she was really concentrating on something unpleasant she drummed on the table with whatever she had handy to release her nervous energy. Finger, pencil, spoon; it didn't matter.

Now she was thinking of how to approach this sad, pitiable man who appeared to be on the edge of a nervous breakdown and ask why he was the last of his kind.

"Tony," she said softly, "Tell me your story. Why are there no other elves, and
why are you here?"

"There are no other elves because they are gone, Ms Caddy. I am here because you woke me up, and I don't have any other place to go to."

Now that was unexpected.

"I woke you up? How did I wake you up?"

"You were singing. Really loud. You were singing to come to you. And I woke up, and if I didn't get out, I'd die. So I got out and went to the Safe Haven, and there were no other elves there at all, and I couldn't stay there, so I came back here to you."

It was all gibberish to Caddy. She had no idea what he was talking about, and he seemed to assume she did. She guessed that it was her drunken singing to the sea a week ago that woke him up, but she had no idea which songs she sang. She was pissed out of her mind. She tried to think of the last time she was so drunk and it was probably when she was 20 and celebrating the day peace was declared at the end of World War Two.

That was also the day she slept with Reggie which led to her six-month "practise marriage" until she found out he was already encumbered with a real live wife. Wild oats best left untended.

This was the second time in her life she got drunk, and both times she ended up with an extra man in the house.

There was a lot to unpack there, and it took all afternoon to draw it out of Tony. He honestly thought she should know everything already and got testy when she kept drilling down for explanations of what to him was obvious. To Tony her questions were like "describe the colour blue." Blue was blue. Why was he asleep? He was hibernating. What is hibernation?
Hibernation is hibernation.

What she eventually learned from Tony was that sometime in the distant past there was a war of genocide and elves were systematically exterminated. To save themselves they had the choice of leaving this world and going into some sort of in-between state of suspended animation, like a hibernation, or staying on the earth and fighting. Tony went into hibernation and woke up to find that there were no elves at all on earth. No one survived.

Tony was the last of his people.

All Caddy could do was sit in horrified silence and absorb what he was telling her. He said there were hundreds of millions of elves in his time before they were slaughtered. He was a banker, he knew his numbers, and Caddy had no reason to doubt Tony's description of the scale
of the mass murder.

When the elves were slaughtered to about ten percent and they saw hope dwindle to nothing, they hatched a plan. They created an in-between place in space and time, and they would go and wait there, in sort of hibernation, until they were awakened. They bet that sooner or later it would be safe to reemerge and that someone would be around to call them back. How they did that, Tony didn't know. That wasn't his department.

Many elves didn't want to go into hibernation and they had their own reasons to reject the plan. Those elves stayed in the world to continue the fight and live with the hope they could stabilise the situation until it was safe enough for their clans to re-emerge. Then they would wake up their fellow elves.

Caddy's drunken song woke Tony. Tony discovered upon awakening that there were no elves alive on the earth. The ones who stayed behind had all died to the last man and woman. He had no sense that there were any elves in hibernation because if Caddy had woken him up, she would have woken them all up. When he woke up he didn't come to Caddy immediately. He went to the Safe Haven and from there he could contact any elf worldwide. But now it was completely empty. There were no elves or elf messages. Nothing.

He figured that he had been asleep for 3,500 years.

Tony was truly and utterly alone, and the only person he could cling to in this new and frightening world was the person who called him up from his deep sleep – and that was Caddy. A Caddy of whom he was obviously terrified.

No wonder he seemed on the verge of a complete mental collapse! Caddy wondered what fraying thread of steel kept the poor man tethered to sanity.

Well, she woke him up and now she was responsible for him. He wasn't the first stray puppy she had taken in, but he was probably the most important and would certainly be the last.

She was old, old, old, and realistically might just have a year or two more. The screwed up cancer diagnosis didn't say she would never die, just that she wasn't going to die *today*.

So she would take the time left to her and her money that no one would inherit and prepare Tony for a day when she was not around. That wouldn't make up for the utter and profound loneliness he would have to endure as the last of his kind, but it might help him endure this new world. She hoped so.

Caddy's decision was made. There was no appeal.

Caddy

Sleep was not Caddy's friend that night. All night long she plotted and planned and made lists, and by the morning she had a rough idea of what to do.

When she walked into the kitchen it was still full dark out and there was no evidence of Tony. For a brief moment she thought he had gone, and she would be left standing there with nothing but memories, outlines, notes, and the strong suspicion that she had imagined it all. But he was sleeping in and when he popped into the kitchen she was sitting at the table with her laptop and an old tablet she had rescued from a drawer.

"Tony, sit here with me!"

But no, he insisted on making her morning coffee and porridge first and finishing some early morning chores, and there was no stopping him without causing a panic attack, so she let him get on with it. In some ways he was a lot like Ricky. In a few days he had developed a routine with systems and procedures, and he wasn't going to deviate from them – for in deviation lies chaos and in chaos lies danger and madness.

When Tony finally was in a place where he could sit at the table and not keep looking over his shoulder at some unfinished task, Caddy smiled at the little man and went into teacher mode.

"Tony, I've been thinking about you all night, and I have some plans."

He blanched. Not good.

"I want you to help me in my shop, but in order to do that you'll need to learn a bit about this world you woke up in. You seem to have figured out this house. How did you do that? How did you learn to use the hob, for instance?"

"I watched you. You turned a knob, and a place on it got hot. When I went to look at it after you left it was all very obvious. And when I dusted I found some instruction manuals on top of the refrigerator."

"You can read!" Caddy was impressed and again Tony was offended.

"Of course, I can read. Interpreting symbols on clay or parchment or paper, it's what I did at the bank every day. You look at the meaning, not the symbol. I don't know why those instruction manuals repeated the same thing four times in four different symbols. That's a bit repetitive."

"So that's how you can speak modern English then. Your brain hears the meaning, not the symbols."

Tony nodded, already getting a bit bored. He looked over his shoulder. There was a closet on the top floor that needed sorting and getting up there made him queasy.

"So Tony, I need you to dress the part. If you go out in public you can't be wearing a toga or whatever that is you have on. You need proper clothes to cover you up and keep you warm."

Miffed, he looked down at himself and fussed with the draping. "I admit this is a bit old, but I haven't had time to make another and from my experience with lords, they don't care. Why do you care what I wear?"

"What's a lord?"

"It's what you are. My lord." Tony sighed. Pretty soon he would be explaining what "up" and "down" were.

Caddy decided to let that one go for now. "Lord" was obviously some sort of social status, like baronet or earl, and if he thought she could tell him what to do, for now that would make things easier for her.

"I care because I want you to feel comfortable and confident in public. I don't want people to focus on your clothes, but on the hard-working, intelligent, professional person that you are."

She didn't say that humans were going to have enough to distract them with his size, not to mention the pointy ears. Talking about people's physical features was rude.

Tony was gobsmacked. Absolutely floored. This lord cared about him. Cared about how he felt. Cared that others had a good opinion of him. This lord thought that he was a hard-working, intelligent, professional person.

This lord said he was a *person*.

What she said was overwhelming and it took a minute to sink in. Caddy thought he was upset about her criticism of his clothes, but he was not. He was prepared for a lord to be dismissive or even cruel. He was not prepared for one to be kind. Kindness knocked the wind out of him.

"What do you want me to do, Ms Caddy?"

"You will learn to use this tablet, and we'll order you some clothes. Tablets are easy to learn, especially for a clever person like you. And while you are learning you can buy some clothes."

And that's what they worked on all morning. She created his own login on the tablet, demonstrated how to swipe and tap a button, showed him how to shop online and to Google for information. And then she let him play on the thing and went over to her own laptop to work on Easter orders.

She thought he'd make a mess of the tablet and get frustrated with it, but what was a computer but a series of symbols? He somehow knew what each icon or squiggle meant and went from there.

He asked a few questions about the type of clothes he needed for the shop and how to measure his size and some questions about colours and style.

"For me, I like British styles of the 1930s to 1950s. That era had the most elegant tailoring, but that's just my opinion. Those were the years I was growing up, so that's probably one reason my taste runs to that time.

But it seems to me that mankind tried out thousands of different styles during the time you were asleep and in 1910 they pretty much hit on what everyone wears now. Trousers, jackets, shirts, dresses. They change in details but not in basic construction. Since 1910, no one has worn bustles or farthingales in everyday fashion, but everyone wears jeans and a t-shirt. If you stick to those eras you'll fit in. Look up "men's clothing 1920" in a search and see what pops up. Choose clothes you like and look comfortable. If it's a mistake, I'll tell you."

Putting together an elf wardrobe was fun. It was like dressing a doll and when she saw his basket she told him to add shoes and underwear and some odds and ends like scarves and hats. Then she showed him how to pay for it with her credit card, which he found to be fascinating, and that led into a conversation on modern electronic banking, credit cards, and many more questions than she could answer.

"You'll have to look those questions up in Google, Tony. I don't know the answers. Just don't believe the first explanation you read.Any idiot can post his thoughts on the internet, so look for consensus of opinion and stay away from individuals with their own crackpot theories.

It will take you a while to learn the difference, so ask me if you have any questions. But right now I need to take a nap."

She gave him the tablet to keep and showed him how to recharge it. Tony became very quiet. Caddy hoped he wasn't afraid of electricity. That wasn't why Tony went quiet; he wasn't afraid of electricity. He was afraid of bonding with this lord who took care of him and gave him such gifts because he was clan-bonding and he knew it. He could feel it. Tony was afraid of finding a family in this woman lord who was so unwell. He was afraid of falling in love.

Caddy and Tony

Amazon delivered a huge pile of boxes and bags the next day, and while the clothes weren't elf-quality, they would do for now. The problem, as Caddy could immediately see, was that while Tony was short, he was not a child, and the child proportions of the clothes he ordered were just not right. He said he could fix that, but what he couldn't fix was the high polyester content of the fabrics. Caddy told him to keep looking, try for more specialist sites, and she would pay for anything he ordered.

"I hope you have enough wardrobe space for all this!" Caddy joked. Considering that all he wore before was one tatty toga, he probably did.

"I don't have a wardrobe, Ms Caddy." He frowned as he folded the clothes and removed the tags. He would have to build one.

"By the way, Tony, where do you live? I've never asked. Is it close by?"

"I live here, Ms Caddy." He looked at her, his face impassive. "In the cellar."

"In the *cellar*! How can you live in the cellar! You can't live in the *cella*r!"

Oh, dear, he thought, now I've done it. I've made her angry. You don't make lords angry. His eyes darted around the room, looking for an escape route.

"But Ms Caddy –" Tony started hyperventilating and he stopped mid-sentence. "I'll move out, right away."

"Damn right you're going to move out. How can you live in the cellar? I have two totally unused bedrooms upstairs. I don't think I've been in either of them for years."

She could only harrumph. "In the cellar! I don't even know where a short guy like you could even put a bed in the cellar. It's damp, and there is no heat and no water."

Caddy jumped up and was irritated at herself for not asking sooner. "You have to show me right now where you are sleeping."

"But Ms Caddy –"

"*Show me, right now, Tony.* This is not a request; it's an order."

Tony

Tony was miserable and terrified at the same time. The lord was furious at him for bedding down in the cellar and she looked at his bed with open disgust.

He had made a nest with some old pillows and towels she had used as paint rags. There was an old milk crate as a table with a few odds and bobs on it, but what really was a kick in the gut for Caddy was the bauble she had given him. It was hanging above his bed like a chandelier. He had it hanging where he had to see it whenever he lay down there.

"You absolutely will not be sleeping down here. I have two free bedrooms upstairs; you choose whichever you want." She turned to the elf. "Tony, you don't deserve to live like this. I won't allow it in my house. I woke you up and you are my responsibility now." And she turned and went back up the stairs.

"Well, are you coming?"

It took a minute, but he choked it out. "Yes, Ms Caddy."

They argued about the bedrooms. Tony didn't want either one. Couldn't he just do some work in the cellar, maybe put some damp proofing in?

"No, thank you very much Ms Caddy, but I just can't sleep that far off the ground. It makes me dizzy. I'll go clean those rooms and fetch stuff if you need it, but I can't sleep up there."

It never occurred to her that Tony was afraid of heights and it never occurred to him that she had no idea about *terrior*.

"I don't know what to do, Tony. I guess I can find you a ground floor flat somewhere nearby. This house used to have a scullery in the kitchen which at least would be warm and dry for you, but it was remodelled into the downstairs loo."

"*Terrior* won't bother me if I'm on the ground floor. It wouldn't bother some elves to sleep on the third floor, but I've always been sensitive, Ms Caddy. Weak stomach, my mum used to say." He looked around the kitchen, and now that he was told about it he could see where the old scullery door was. "Ms Caddy, if I can figure something out here would you mind?"

"You do whatever you want, Tony. My knees would really miss the downstairs loo if I have to keep going upstairs to pee, but if it needs to go to get you out of the cellar, then it goes." She took a sip of her tea. "I can still look for a flat. I had no idea you had a terror of heights."

"Not terror, Ms Caddy, *terrior*."

"Ok, what's *terrior*? And stop rolling your eyes at me, Tony. I really don't know. You're my first elf, and you didn't come with an instruction manual."

"Ms Caddy, all elves are tied to the land we are born on. We take –" And he hesitated; this was so hard to explain, and he was a numbers guy, not a words guy. " – energy from the earth and each place has its own mix of minerals, water, air, and energy. That mix is vital to us to live. That's why we live in houses that are partly underground. It's healthier for us."

"Your cellar is damp and nasty, but that's not how our houses are. They're warm and cosy and dry, but I could fix up the cellar, given time."

"When I go to the third floor and stay too long I get nauseated. I read on the tablet about human aeroplanes. I could never go on an aeroplane, Ms Caddy. I would literally die. Any elf would, not just those of us with sensitive stomachs."

"Heavens, Tony, I had no idea. I just don't want you to live in squalor, that's just not on. Could you turn the cellar into an elf house? If you can make it warm, dry, and cosy like an elf house, it's all yours. "

Tony gave a sigh of relief and for the first time Caddy saw him smile. Really smile.

"And use my credit card, dear. Get whatever you need."

The new year came and went, and Tony worked on his cellar home and took care of Caddy. Caddy, for her part, worked on pre-orders for the shop and took care of Tony, mostly by providing her credit card. She had no idea what was going on in the cellar, but given the amount of noise, it must have been significant. When she offered to hire in some tradesmen to do things like the electrics Tony was quite emphatic that he could do it all himself. After all, if he had any questions or needed any lessons he had his tablet and YouTube to fall back on.

Caddy crossed her fingers and hoped he wouldn't burn the house down.

After Twelfth Night, Caddy returned to the shop to take down the Christmas decor and get ready for this year's Easter decorations to be shipped in. She showed Tony how to run the till, and that led her into showing Tony her accounting and inventory system. That in turn was either a huge mistake or a huge boon, depending on how you look at it. He just took it over.

"THIS, Ms Caddy, is what I *do*!" She had never seen anyone so excited over accounting in all her days. Learning His Majesty's Revenue & Customs tax rules, checking her bank statements, reading accounting textbooks, and learning her computer systems – it was all entertainment to Tony and a welcome relief from dusting and cooking porridge.

She threw her hands up and passed over all the back end of the shop and her bank accounts to Tony. Caddy was quite capable of managing the boring bits, but that didn't mean she liked it.

The other reason was, when you got down to it, she was very old and if he was going to take over everything after she passed on he needed to learn how to work in modern human society. She didn't want her elf to go to jail for tax evasion. Not that the taxman could arrest him – Tony would just pop away. But, it would be a bother.

Every year sometime between the 15th and 20th of January Caddy reopened the shop. The night before this year's reopening, she sat down to dinner with Tony and without warning told him, "I need to call my solicitor tomorrow. Don't let me forget."

They were having takeaway tonight, Kentucky Fried Chicken, and Tony was munching on a drumstick that looked massive in his hands. "What for, Ms Caddy? Are you still worried about that lease? I thought it was all taken care of."

"I want to update my will. I need to get Lizzie taken off and you put down in her place."

Tony put down the chicken leg, shocked. "You're going to remove your daughter?"

"She's dead, Tony. She's been gone for two years now. She doesn't need any of my chattels or bank accounts." Caddy didn't look up. "You, on the other hand, do. When I pass on, as we all inevitably do, I want everything to go to you."

Tony started to cry. He didn't make a sound, but fat streams of water ran down his thin cheeks. Caddy leaned forward and patted his greasy hand.

"Oh, don't be sad. I've had an extraordinarily long life for a human. I don't mind the end coming. You, on the other hand, have just woken up to a new world. You need my crap much more than I do. I have eleven egg cups in my egg cup collection. Think about what you can do with that!"

Tony looked at Caddy as if she were mad.

"But you're a lord, Ms Caddy. You're not going to die."

"Tony, we all die, I'm afraid. You yourself said all the elves were dead. Were there lords back then, too? What happened to them?"

"They were killed, Ms Caddy. Anyone can be killed; that's true. Or have an accident. But that's not the same as dying of old age. Lords will live forever if they are not killed."

Caddy pointed a french fry at the elf and totally ignored the lord nonsense. "I was born in 1925, Mr Tony. That was a long, long time ago. Very few people live past 100, and I've far exceeded that."

"I'm 947 years old, Ms Caddy, and that doesn't include the hibernation time."

Caddy was shocked. "Nine hundred and forty seven! Goodness! How long do elves live? Do you live forever?"

"No, we don't live forever. We live for about three thousand years or so."

"So it just seems like forever." Caddy smiled. "Do you get as decrepit as a human or do you stay young the entire time?"

"We stay pretty healthy to the end and then we just fall over and die."

"The best way to go. That's how Ricky went. No pain, no wasting away." She pushed away her plate. She used to never eat more than one or two pieces of chicken and today she gobbled down four.

"But if you have two thousand more years to go, you'll need some assets and that's why I'm changing my will."

"Ms Caddy, I don't want to live another two thousand years alone, without my clan or without you as my lord. So you have to do your best to stay alive."

Caddy grinned at the little man. "I will do my best, Tony. So far I've been successful."

_____

Caddy

"Ms Caddy, I don't want to live another two thousand years alone…"

That was the saddest thing she had ever heard.

Caddy and Tony

It was raining. Not the usual just-enough-to-be-annoying Lowestoft rain, but really
tipping down.

Caddy sat in the shop, but she knew there wouldn't be any customers coming in, not in this mess. Tony was sitting next to her on the stool, typing something on his tablet. It looked boring. She glanced at her weather app on her phone, hoping against hope that there would be a break in the weather so she didn't have to ride her bike home and get soaked through.

"I wish I could port like you do, Tony. I sure don't want to ride home in this."

Porting was what Tony called the ability he had to disappear and reappear somewhere else.

"I can port you home, Ms Caddy. All you have to do is ask."

Caddy put her phone away and turned to the elf. "You never told me you could port me!"

"You never asked. Porting is something elves have always done for lords. It's one reason they keep us around. "

"Port me now. Send me home." And she squeezed her eyes shut and waited.

"That's not how it works, Ms Caddy-Lazybones. You have to get up and walk. I'll make a porthole, and you walk through it." Reluctantly, he saved the stew of numbers on the tablet, jumped down from the stool, and pointed, "The hole is going to be over here, and please don't dither. Walk right through the hole. It's hard to hold open."

"Let's do it!" She jumped up. Tony simply stared at a space, and an oval appeared. It was edged in black smoke and the centre was grey smoke with tiny sparks in it. She didn't hesitate, because she trusted Tony, and he had told her not to dither, but oh, was that first port a literal leap of faith! Like a doorway, Caddy just walked through it.

And she was in her sitting room. There was a snapping sound, and Tony was standing next to her, an eyebrow cocked.

"Easy peasy!"

"Oh, I want to go back now." Another circle was made, she walked through it, and just like that she was back in the shop.

"Amazing!" Caddy was delighted, and her happiness made Tony smile. "How far can you go? Can I go to London? I haven't been to the V&A for years!"

"No, I can only port in my clan area. About 30 miles is as far as I can go if I'm feeling really good that day. Some elves can port twice that, but I'm not an athlete. Lords port long distances by using relays of elves. Each one of us has our area, but our areas overlap. "

And since there are no other elves – Caddy filled in the rest. No trips to the museums.
No V&A.

"But you can port to Safe Haven. You told me that. I'm pretty sure Safe Haven isn't here in Suffolk."

"Any elf can port to Safe Haven, Ms Caddy. It's neither here nor there, and there are no distance restrictions. That's how an elf can meet and talk with elves all over the world. An elf from Stockholm can physically meet with an elf from Pretoria in the Safe Haven, but never on this Earth."

"Can you port me to the Safe Haven?"

"Fuck no! Are you crazy?" The elf's head spun around, making sure no one heard the demented lord.

"No need to get salty with me, Tony! Why am I crazy?"

"*No one* but elves go to Safe Haven. That's why it's a safe haven. The *only* tribe allowed in there are elves. No humans, no lords, and certainly no orcs."

Orcs? Another question for later.

"Then why didn't all the elves go there instead of going into hibernation? That seems the obvious answer to me."

"Because Safe Haven has no *terrior*. It's a sterile place. We need our patches of dirt or we get sick. My mum used to say that Safe Haven was like sweets. One day is fine. Too much and you'll get sick." Tony looked at his feet. "Some tried. They would port to Safe Haven and stay for a while in hiding, then port back to stay in their homes when staying in Safe Haven made them sick."

His voice fell to a whisper. "But they were waiting, Ms Caddy. They went for the children first."

Caddy winced. She could imagine the horror of taking a sick child to the only place you knew they'd get well and then –

She was afraid to ask what happened to them.

"We knew we couldn't stay there even before we tried." He shrugged. "Each clan has – had – a huge pot of their own dirt with a clan totem in it. They looked sort of like those big pots on the Prom, the ones with flowers and a signpost in them.

If you were feeling a bit queasy or hung over, you could go there, have a sit, and get better. They were filled with flowers and we refreshed our pots' soil every season. Safe Haven is covered with pots, thousands and thousands of them. That's how I know I'm the last elf. Every single pot is sterile and dead. No one is tending their pot. It's a grey, dead world."

"If it's a dead world, Tony, then you can make the rules. And you can break them. So why can't I go there?"

"Because I didn't make the place and set the rules, Ms Caddy. Safe Haven was made as a place to escape from humans, orcs, and lords. If I take you there, I don't know what will happen to you. Or to me for trying. Something horrible, I'm sure, so I won't do it. Anyway, I'm not ever going back there."

Tony casually walked to the other end of the shop and straightened up a display of snow globes. He knew it was silly to feel that way with Ms Caddy, but he was brought up knowing that telling a lord no was dangerous. Better safe than sorry, as mum would say.

She nodded and let the matter drop. It was a dead-end conversation about a dead world, so no point in making Tony more upset. Instead she asked what was for dinner and that was a welcome change of subject for the elf. It was time, anyway, to close up shop and he ported them both back home, warm and dry.

But all through dinner she kept thinking about the Safe Haven. She was missing a trick; she could feel it. It was right there at the edge of her brain, like a forgotten name of a casual acquaintance, but she couldn't place it. It would come to her, though.

Ellen

"Good morning, Ms Caddy!"

Caddy was unpacking a box of tin eggs for the Easter display when she looked up to see Ellen walk through the door.

"Ellen! As radiant as always! It's so nice to see you!" And they hugged and made all the girly twittering and cooing noises old friends make when they meet up.

Ellen took a good look at her Ms Caddy. Then she looked again, startled. Ms Caddy was exactly like Ellen remembered when she was a child, and how old must Ms Caddy have been then? In her eighties? In the last few years she had noticed, with sadness, that her old friend was getting frail, which was to be expected when you're over a hundred years old. Oh, when you walked in the shop she always greeted you with a musical hello! And she bustled around like a caffeinated hummingbird, but while most of her customers wouldn't notice it, Ellen had seen her slow down in the last few years, especially after Lizzie died. Lizzie's death took some of the old Ms Caddy sparkle away.

But today's Ms Caddy was a different woman compared to the one who talked with the doctor and her unfortunate boss during Ellen's visit last November. Whatever Ms Caddy was drinking she needed to bottle it because the woman – while still white-haired, built like a barrel, and wrinkled as an old raisin – looked like she had dropped twenty years. She looked healthy.

"So, Ellen, what brings you here today? Business or pleasure?"

"A bit of both, Ms Caddy. First, here's a card for your birthday. Happy Birthday!" And she handed Caddy a card.

"Thank you! Now you haven't told anyone, have you?"

"No, ma'am. You told me at 100 not to ever let anyone know because you didn't want to have one of those photo-ops in the paper. So I haven't. "

"Good girl! And thank you for the card; it's lovely."

"It's a picture of a hundred-year-old going up in flames from birthday candles, Ms Caddy."

"Yes, I can see that, dear. It's perfect." Caddy smiled and gave Ellen a kiss on the cheek. "I'll treasure it always."

"You'll throw it away as soon as I leave the shop."

"Yes, of course I will. So what is the business that brings you here? Tell me the bad news, and then I have some good news for you!"

"It's not bad news; it's just business. Dr Crowe has signed off that you are healthy and mentally able to manage your own affairs and closed down any inquiries about you. But Mr Assam has put a note in your file that I am to visit you once a month, *alone*, to make sure you don't go off the rails and we get blamed for letting you fall through the cracks. That's why I'm here."

"Oh, that's not bad, not at all. If you came over once a month for tea as a part of your official duties that would be brilliant! Now –" and Caddy grinned. Ellen swore later she saw a mischievous glint of green in the old woman's eyes. "I would like to introduce you to a new friend of mine. Tony!!" And she turned to her right to look at – nothing.

Ellen waited, curious. What was Ms Caddy up to? Who was Tony?

No Tony appeared.

"Tony! Please come here. I want you to meet Ellen!"

Nothing.

Ellen looked at Caddy, who was getting cross and frowning at something behind the counter.

Oh dear, Ellen thought, and instant tears filled her eyes. Poor Ms Caddy.

"Tony, this is a direct order!"

Nothing.

Then, from behind the curtain shuffled out the tiniest, most doleful man Ellen had ever seen. He was perfectly proportioned and wearing grey tweed trousers with braces, a white cotton shirt buttoned to the collar, and a dark grey flat cap which didn't hide his pointy ears.

Pointy ears.

The man was one metre tall.

With pointy ears.

Caddy smiled at Tony, this time with sympathy.

"Tony, this is my very good friend Ellen. Ellen, this is my very good friend Tony."

Tony looked at Ellen. Ellen looked at Tony. He tried to smile, but Ellen could see he was down-to-the-ground terrified, and she had a blinding flash of self-awareness. She was a very, very tall, very, very curvaceous woman and must look huge to this very, very small man.

"It's good to meet you, Tony. Any friend of Ms Caddy is my friend, too. She's a wonderful judge of character." And she held out her hand and bent a low as was dignified and practical. Thank goodness she was wearing a high-necked jumper.

Tony reached out and shook the offered hand. Once. When she let go he couldn't help but look at his hand as if relieved to have it back intact.

"It's good to meet you, too, Ms Ellen. Ms Caddy always speaks well of you."

They stared at each other.

Caddy smiled at both of her favourite people. It went as well as can be expected, she thought.

"There! Introductions have been made. Ellen, if you don't mind, Tony has some work he's finishing up, and he'd like to get back to it."

"Of course. Thank you for coming out to meet me, Tony."

"It was nice to meet you, too, Ellen." With obvious relief on his face, Tony took a step back and ported out with a snap, making Ellen jump.

She turned to Caddy and for a minute she couldn't talk.

"Ms Caddy, he –"

"Tony lives with me and occasionally works in the shop." Caddy beamed. "He's an elf, but we don't dwell on that. I don't discriminate based on race, religion, gender, or tribe. He's simply a wonderful person."

"An elf."

"Of course. What else can he be?" Then Caddy grinned and touched Ellen on the nose with the tip of her finger. "But we're not going to talk about *that* in public either, are we? Just put down in your report that I now have live-in help."

"Yes ma'am."

Tony and Caddy

"You didn't tell me you were going to introduce me to Ms Ellen." Tony's tone was accusatory.

"No, I didn't know she was coming in. The shop was empty, and it seemed to be the right moment." Caddy's tone was conciliatory.

"She's a human."

"And you're an elf." Caddy knew they had to hash this out. "Tony, if you're going to live in this world with me you have to interact with humans. You need to learn how to manage them. Yes, I know some humans are awful people who do terrible things. But some are not. They are easily led, I think. So our job is to sort out the good ones from the bad ones."

Caddy patted his hand. "Don't forget I'm human, my friend. Am I so bad?"

They were eating dinner, and Tony scowled into his kung pao noodles. "You're a lord, Ms Caddy. You're not a human."

"I was born to a human mother and father Tony. I've had human children fathered by a human man. If it walks like a duck –"

"Doesn't make you human, Ms Caddy."

Caddy stifled a sigh. She really didn't understand why he was saying that. Couldn't she be a lord and a human being? She could be a dame and a human being. She could be a fekkin' queen and a human being.

"I don't understand and I think you need to go back to basics and explain to me how your world works. Remember, Tony, I really have no idea about your elf world – why people in the distant past fought each other and who all the major players are. I was born in this time and place, and that's *all* I know. It's like I've walked into the last ten minutes of a football game and I don't know the players, who's on what team or the rules of the game are."

She looked at Tony, "Let's start with this one – whenever you talked about who can and cannot go to Safe Haven you mentioned elves, lords, humans, and trolls. Why them?"

"Orcs, Ms Caddy, not trolls. Trolls don't exist."

"Good! It is now established that I don't have to think about trolls. Talk to me about what I do have to think about."

He looked at his noodles and then, with a sigh, pushed them away and instead took a
drink of his beer.

"There are four great tribes in the world. There are elves, humans, lords, and orcs. The tribes are balanced with their opposites, more or less. Elves partner with lords, and humans
partner with orcs.

"I'm an elf. I can port and do certain things that you call magic and I call abilities. I'm able to do some things no human, orc, or lord can do. My dis-ability is that I'm tied to the soil I was born in. I'm very powerful inside of my world, but I can't leave it. I'm mortal. I have a very long lifespan, but it will end. I will, if I'm lucky and find the right woman, have only four or five children in my entire life. We can only make babies if we have a lord around."

Caddy nodded, she knew most of that. The baby part was weird. Did she have to watch?

"Humans, on the other hand, are very clever. They don't do magic, but they can invent machines that imitate magic. They can go anywhere they want, even to the moon! They have short lives, only about 100 years, but they can have many, many children to take their places. I read on the internet that one woman had 69 children!"

"That's not typical, Tony, but point taken."

Tony began to tick off the facts with this fingers, "Humans can interbreed with lords and orcs. I don't think they can tell the difference, really. They'll screw anyone.

Orcs don't do magic, as such, but they have some magical physical properties. They can go anywhere. They are very strong and can heal from just about any injury. To really kill an orc you have to cut off his head. Everything else you can do to him just heals or grows back. They're not clever, but they are very persuasive and manipulative, and some of that is more than just words. Orcs live the shortest time, only about 70 years, but they reproduce as fast as humans, maybe faster. Very few orcs are born as singletons. Most orcs are part of twins and triplets. Orcs can take anything apart. Anything. But they can't build anything. They can't see cause and effect and can't plan, so they often make stupid decisions.

Humans and orcs work together because orcs need humans to plan and do clever things. And humans – well I don't think they need orcs as much as some of them want to use them for their own purposes. Orcs use their powers of persuasion to get humans to do things for them.

And that leaves lords. Lords can go anywhere in the world. They are magic, but they can't port like an elf. Some are strong in their abilities; some are much weaker. They can all move things a bit, like you do, Ms Caddy, but there are also a very few who can do something really huge like control fire or water. Most though do one thing like heal flesh or make things freeze. Some can change their shape, but it's dangerous for them so they don't do it very often. Lords live forever unless they are killed or commit suicide. They don't have many children. Most never do. Back in my time lords helped the elves, and elves helped the lords. We kept them healthy and ported them around, and they, in turn, protected us when we needed it and gave us Scent.

Then the world went crazy. It went out of balance when Gaia committed suicide and in doing so killed all of the strongest lords. That left weak ones, and in the unbalance the orcs and humans thought they would teach the snobby, selfish lords a lesson, and they went and killed every weak one they could find.

The elves tried to protect the lords; we need them to survive. So the orcs and humans killed the elves off, too. The world is now unbalanced, tilted to humans and orcs and they have taken over everything."

Tony fell silent and Caddy sat silent, too. Thinking.

"That's a lot to absorb, Tony. I'll have more questions tomorrow."

"I'm sure you will, Ms Caddy." Tony smiled ruefully. "I understand tomorrow is your birthday."

"Yes, it is! Another year to add to the total. I was born February 2, 1925. Candlemas Day to Christians and Imbolc to the old religion." Caddy smiled. "Ricky once told me that the day I was born was the end of winter and the beginning of spring, which I thought was a lovely compliment."

So Tony thought she was a lord, probably because she could move things. Caddy was not convinced, mostly because she was so darn old. If lords were this decrepit at 100, what were they like at 1,000? He also said lords could be killed or kill themselves. She thought about her stupid suicide attempt and how the sea spit her back onto land like a piece of rotten fruit.

It would certainly be ironic if the only lord in this world had died as a result of a computer systems error at the National Health Service.

But the concept of balance – that felt so right, so elementally correct, that Caddy simply had to accept that. Today's world was not in balance because two of the four great tribes were missing. There was absolutely nothing she could do about that, but it certainly explained a lot of what she saw in history right up to today's news.

Caddy and Tony

The cake was beautiful, as was everything Tony made. It was chocolate – Caddy's favourite – and it had cream and coffee frosting on it. He didn't put a candle on it for each year so there was no chance of burning down the kitchen, but he did put a sparkler in the centre which added a festive touch.

Caddy ate two huge pieces and drank a big glass of wine, and if that wasn't going to put her in a sugar coma nothing would.

She patted her stomach and laughed. "Tony, you're going to make me very fat. I can't seem to get enough food in, but with your cooking I'm trying!"

"It's the abilities practise, Ms Caddy, that is making you hungry. You're burning up a lot of energy, and I have to keep you fed to replace it. It's all to the good. Working your abilities makes you stronger and healthier. I was really worried when I first saw you, but now you're looking a lot better. You're a lord, Ms Caddy. Lords need to practise their abilities because it makes them healthy much like humans need to exercise to stay healthy."

Tony cleared the plates off the table, and Caddy stacked them in the dishwasher, listening as he spoke. "You told me that you moved that first bauble just a few weeks before you woke me up. You're still a baby in lord terms."

"Tony, you should wish me many happy returns of the day."

"I certainly do, ma'am."

She turned to him and leaned on the counter, wiping her hands dry on a Rum Lot tea towel.

"Now I have a birthday wish that only you can give me."

Tony was immediately suspicious. She had that glint in her eye that meant trouble.

"What's that, Ms Caddy?"

"Tony, I want you to go to Safe Haven and do two things. I want you to go and look at the pots and make double sure that each one is dead. No fresh earth, no plants – 3,500 years of dead. If you find one alive, you have to tell me. If you find any evidence that lords, orcs, or humans have been there, you have to tell me. I want to know that for 3,500 years, since the last time an elf was on this earth, Safe Haven has been deserted. And I want something, anything, brought back from there that will prove you were there. That's it."

The elf's face was paper white. *That's it?* That's all she wanted? That he return to a place he used to love and now was hell?

"Don't make me go back, Ms Caddy! Please!"

Caddy was solemn, and her eyes were bright with tears. She knew this would cost him, but she was firm.

"We have to be sure that no elves now exist and that in 3,500 years they didn't wake up and go somewhere else." She squatted down to be eye-to-eye with the elf.

"Tony, I think you're wrong, I think you were so upset and exhausted the last time you were there you didn't think it through. If the place is dead, and it's the ONLY place the rest of the elves could be, then they must still be hibernating. If they are still hibernating and I woke up one, maybe I can wake up more."

"Tony, you might not be the last elf; you might be the first elf."

She stood back up and smiled. "Bring me back a birthday present, Tony. And if you can, tell me that there is no evidence of any elf or anyone else being there for 3,500 years. Because that's what I want to hear."

Without a word, Tony ported out.

_____

Tony

Stunned. He couldn't breathe.

Tony didn't go to Safe Haven; he went to the toilet.

There he sat and tried to create some order to the whirlwind of chaos in his brain and think through what the lord had said. When you looked at it her way, the lack of evidence of any elves in Safe Haven was a good thing. It meant they were still in hibernation. He had taken the desolation of a place that should be a heaving mass of elves as evidence that they were all dead.

The more he thought about it, the more he had to admit that he had jumped to a conclusion without real evidence. She wanted evidence, one way or the other, and she was going to make him go get it.

Lords commanded, elves obeyed.

He had a direct order.

_____

Tony

No wind. No sound. Just absolute stillness and absolute silence because it takes
life to make both.

In the living world death means decay. Life is balanced by death, and everything cycles from one to the other. Whether life dances in the shape of a whale or in the formless blob of a slime mould, it is born, it lives, it divides or releases copies of itself, and then it dies, its body dissolving into atoms which coalesce to create new life. The sine wave of life is always moving from the peaks of living to the valleys of death. Safe Haven was neither growing nor decaying; it had flatlined.

Safe Haven was in perfect balance, and being in perfect balance meant it was dead.

Tony stood in the main square, a place he had stood hundreds of times Before. Then it was a heaving, chaotic mass of busy, happy, sad, hurried, chattering, greeting, goodbye-ing elves. Elves from all over the world would come in to visit, to meet, to trade, to move things.

The very centre of the square was a tall spire called The Point that could be seen across the entire Safe Haven. It was elaborately carved and had no real utility other than it was pretty and a meeting place.

How many times had someone said to Tony, "We'll meet at The Point at such and such a time, and we'll go to the pub?" Every lost child knew that all he had to do was look in the skyline and see the point and make his way there and someone in his clan would find him sooner or later.

Today the square was empty. It was an eerie stage set devoid of movement and where Tony had interpreted that silence and emptiness as death, now it felt more like waiting.

He walked through the square and past the stalls that lined it and the rows of pubs, inns, and meeting houses. The entire Safe Haven was a massive transit zone, not a village. People didn't live there any more than people live in Heathrow or any of the great train stations of the world. The place was chock-a-block with hotels, B&Bs, and inns for every elf taste and they reflected every region of the world.

Back then, there was no uniform elven culture any more than there is a uniform human culture, so elves from what is now the African continent had places to stay that suited their taste or they stayed at an inn from a different culture for variety the way humans travelled to exotic lands to experience novelty.

Tony had his favourite haunts, and that's where he headed to now. He went to the Plough and Sail, *his* pub and inn where he lodged when he stayed overnight.

Overnights were with Elisa. Always with Elisa. He had no reason to stay the night when it was just as easy to port home to his parent's house but every reason to spend the night with Elisa.

As he walked through the alleyways and streets he examined every pot of soil he passed by. He knew the clans; he could read the totems and it was heart-wrenching. Some had messages written on bits of metal or wood poked in the soil – messages in Elvish that said things like, "Eric of the Littor Clan, if you read this I have gone home to fight. Wish me luck!" or "Judith, we are all going into hibernation on the morrow. We love you." Or even "To Michel of Balorick, Your order of three pairs of trousers is waiting for you at The Goose. Our shop is now closed for the foreseeable future."

The most heart-wrenching notes were from parents looking for their children. Tony couldn't read those at all.

Many of the notes were dated, but after a certain date there were no messages at all. He didn't see any evidence at all that anyone had left a note or a memorial message in the intervening 3,500 years.

The plants in the huge pots were all dead. They had struggled for a while untended, and Tony could see that, but in the end lack of water and no fresh soil had dried them into perfect mummies of themselves. With no insects or wind to help with pollinating there were no seeds. With no wind or rain there was no erosion and recycling and so the flowers, trees, and bushes stood where they died, frozen in time. If Tony brushed by too close and created the faintest of winds they dissolved into tiny particles of dust.

When Tony saw that they dissolved with a touch or the slightest of breezes he looked for evidence that others had come by and saw nothing. He was the only one who made the flowers dissolve into dust.

His breath quickened as his heart raced. No evidence. No evidence that any elf had been here after hibernating. He started to run, and as he ran, his boots echoed on the cobbles and the sound waves and the breeze he made by moving through the air made the most delicate of the flowers disintegrate into their component atoms and fall onto the sterile soil.

Then it appeared, the old familiar alley with the Plough and Sail at the corner. There were benches and tables sitting in front, as there always were, and some long-gone elf had gathered some tankards on a tray and then left it there. Someone had a last drink. Some three. And they didn't bother to take the tankards back to the kitchen, something an elf would never do, not if it was in normal times. This neglected tray wasn't evidence of a hurried exit, it was evidence of despair. Why bother taking dirty tankards back to the kitchen? Who would see them? Who would need a clean tankard later? Ever?

Tony pushed the door open and walked inside. It was as if the last bell had been rung, and the bar was closed for the evening. The main room was wiped down and ready for the next day's trade, and in the last 3,500 years there had been no dust to worry about because there had been no life to make it and no activity to stir it up. The place gleamed with old polished wood, and on dark painted walls the frescos told stories of sailing ships and farmers in their fields. He remembered one fresco, and there it was – a stall of elf farmers at a busy market selling apples, and in the crowd were elves, two lords, humans, and orcs. No one was fighting. No one was hating. Even the orcs were waiting their turn at the apple stall, although the fresco did show one picking the pocket of a human woman.

How did it all go so wrong?

He went up the narrow stairs to the sleeping rooms above and stood outside the second door on the left, his heart racing and breaking at the same time.

This was Elise's favourite room and the one they always booked when they were on their dates. She had bonded with him the minute they had their first words together. Goodness knows what they talked about. He had no clue. Probably an accounting question.

But he hadn't bonded with Elise.

Bonding is a funny thing. One person can bond and the other won't or can't, and while that's sad for the bonder, it's pretty much neutral for the bond-ee. Flattering, but no heart will be broken if the spark isn't there.

Over time, though, sometimes things change. Elise loved Tony with all her heart, but she was wise enough to understand that didn't mean he loved her in return and that he had to come around in his own time, if ever. She was patient.

She met him while working on projects, and then one day after a meeting here in Safe Haven he asked if she would like to share a table at the pub. She was attractive, but not beautiful, but then neither was he. While he didn't have instant lust for her, she was pleasant, and he had grown to enjoy her company. A few meetings later and a few shared dinners later and they were sharing a bed.

He grew to appreciate her wit and admire her accounting acumen. That sounds odd; he knew that, but all bonds are based on respect, and he respected her long before he loved her. Then, gradually, he found that lust and respect and shared experiences and laughter added up to much more than the sum of their parts. The accounting books of love and bonding always came to a surprising bottom line. They never added up.

So he did the sums and thought a long time and then asked her if they should set up a house together and she agreed. They argued over the exact place. She lived in Ipswich, and he lived in Lowestoft, and because of *terrior* they decided on a place in the middle. Choosing a place to share their lives was of utmost importance to elves because their children would be bound to that soil so they needed to be close to both clans. And then there was the matter of good schools and such.

But then it all went to hell.

The orcs and humans came in waves to overwhelm and destroy the elves. They first rose up in the west, in what is now the Birmingham area, and spread out like an ugly stain from there. Lords were gone, dead or destroyed or just lost, so they couldn't put the invaders back in their proper place and reset the balance. With each terrible wave the remaining elves did what they could to survive, and then the horde reached London. The London clans went to ground early, but the outlying areas were slow. They just couldn't believe what was happening. They tried different ways to repel the hordes, but eventually, one by one, each clan household, farm, and village fought on its own, in their own way and each in turn was lost.

Tony was at work when he heard Elise die. It wasn't a scream, it was her sudden and complete absence that he heard. He looked up, confused, and started looking for her, but since she was dead, there was nothing to sense, nothing to hear. The elf that was Elise was now just an empty hole in his heart.

He had to look for her the human way, which meant physically going from location to location to find her. With each port and each empty room he became more and more frantic.

Suddenly, he remembered that she was looking at a house on her uncle's farm, and it took him ages to look up the location so he could port there. Hill Farm, Chediston.

He found her. She and her uncle's family were all dead. Slaughtered and half eaten by the orcs who feasted on the elf family the way they feasted on chaos and death. They gorged until they could eat no more, and then left the half-chewed body parts where they fell, in filth and anarchy.

The pyre wasn't huge, but he did the best he could. He gathered up all the remains he could find before the crows and gulls got to them and did his best to send funny, beautiful, beloved Elise respectfully into the Void. He hoped she would be reborn to a happier world. He hoped she would find a man who loved her the way he should have from the start and the way he did at the end, when it was too late.

Then he went into hibernation. When Caddy woke him up, Tony had been awake three days since Elise was murdered. It was as if the intervening 3,500 years had never happened and to his raw, wounded heart, her death was yesterday.

Tony

Tony stood outside the second door on the left and then turned and went back downstairs. The more he prayed to and grieved Elise the longer she would wait in the Void, listening to him and sharing his pain. He wouldn't put her through that. That was selfish, and she deserved better. If he was slow to love her when he had the chance he would love her the best way he could now that she was dead, and that meant releasing her.

He had work to do.

Tony wandered in and out of the little shops thinking that if anyone had come by in the last 3,500 years they would have scavenged goods to take back to wherever they were hiding. The shops weren't full, but what scavenging had been done was completed between the time elves went into hibernation and the final eradication of elves on Earth.

Then he found an elf. He walked into a chandler's shop, and sitting behind the counter, exactly the way Caddy sat behind her shop counter, was an elf.

Searching hard for elves and coming up empty and then next minute suddenly seeing another person scared the stuffing out of Tony, and for a wild minute he didn't know if he should run up to the man and give him a hug or run out of the shop screaming.

The chandler was a chubby man but one who had that deflated look that comes with losing weight much too fast. In his hand was a quill, and he was writing. He was as dead as the flowers and trees outside. Tony crept up and looked closely, afraid to breathe and make the dead man disintegrate like the plants in the clan pots did. But he couldn't help himself, and some breath or tremor or flutter of his eyelash and the death shadow of the man collapsed, and there was nothing left but a pile of sand and dust in a heap of ancient clothes.

The letter was two parts. The top part was from the man's son saying he would be there soon, and they would go to hibernation together where the rest of the family was already waiting. The second part was the message the chandler was leaving for his son. He was getting *terrior* sick and had to go, but he would wait as long as he could. The son never came. The man never left.

The next shops were more of the same, but now Tony looked for something for Caddy to prove he had been there. His heart told him that no proof was necessary, but that's what she said, and that's what he would do. Now he understood why she made him do this terrible journey. If he hadn't returned he would always think that no one made it out alive but himself. But while Safe Haven looked dead, it wasn't dead. It was like the chandler. It was waiting.

He found a pair of proper elf-made boots for himself, and for her he found a box set of beautiful elf-knives. You couldn't buy those on Amazon! He could always come back if he needed something, but surely she would never make him take this trip again.

_____

Caddy and Tony

"I want you to go back," she said as the lord sat at the kitchen table and examined the elf knives. He had reported to her everything he saw and felt and how Safe Haven was a dead place but a waiting place, too.

"Ms Caddy! I –"

"I want you to go and set up a clan pot near that spire you were talking about. I want it full of good Suffolk dirt, your choice of location, and I want it planted with bright flowers. Personally, I'm partial to pink geraniums, but you do what you want. Pansies are good.
Which do you like better?"

"Ms Caddy!"

"And then I want you to go there once a week and water them. I want a big fekkin' sign in the middle telling whoever walks by where we are and some extra writing tools and that sort of thing so messages can be sent." She examined the box the knives came in. Beautiful.

"If I can figure out how to wake up more of you, I have no idea where they will come from and where they will go. We will be learning this process for a long time, and I have no clue how elf-waking is supposed to work. For all I know I could wake up a whole village of elves in Botswana and not know it. The first thing they will do, I gather, is go to Safe Haven, and so we must connect with them that way. That's why I want you to do this. I want you to plant a signpost that says we are here. I don't want the next elf who ports to Save Haven to think he's the only elf alive."

She looked over the box at the elf.

"Can you do all that Tony?"

"Yes ma'am, you know I can."

"Do you want to do all that Tony?"

"*No!* Maybe." He paused. "Actually, I think I do."

"Good! I thought you would! Best get cracking then!" She looked at the knives again and awkwardly pulled one out and Tony was sure in his bones she was going to cut herself.

"These are lovely, Tony. I think this is going to be my best birthday present ever. I really do."

Jack

The raven flew in long lazy loops over Lowestoft looking for his hen. There was a big wind last night and she blew off course. And while she was as intelligent as she was beautiful, he was surprised she found her way out of the egg. She couldn't direction-find worth a crap.

Jack (his name was Jack One-Eye) was pretty sure she would have enough sense not to go over the water to France, so when he realised she was missing and knowing the direction of the winds, he left Kent and started flying north. Jack decided when he got to Great Yarmouth he would start back. Surely she wouldn't go any further.

He landed on a chimney pot to rest a minute and gave a huge squawk just in case she was nearby. All he did was startle some nesting herring gulls into making a huge ruckus, but they didn't seem to disturb anyone on the street, not even the elf doing some very early morning gardening.

There was an elf.

He was gardening.

The gardener was an elf.

Jack couldn't swear-word believe his one eye. He looked, he cocked his head, he poo'd, and then he flew down to sit on the low iron railings mounted on the wall that surrounded the garden.

The elf ignored him as would anyone who thought birds were birds and that a very big raven in Suffolk was normal. It was not. Ravens lived in the western part of England, and it was rare to see them on the North Sea side. Normally Jack lived in the Kent Downs and never ventured this far north. If it wasn't for the mis-directed hen he would never have come to Lowestoft, and he would never have seen the elf.

And then, *miracle des dieux*, out of the door walked a lord who said something to the elf. A lord!! A rather ragged-looking to be sure, female lord. She stopped, looked across the small patch of garden directly at Jack, frowned, shrugged, and went back inside.

Jack was beside himself. He squawked and squawked, and his hen was suddenly at his side, wanting to know what his problem was. Was he lost?

Jack

Jack called the hen Jill, for some unknown reason. And the hen answered to it even though it wasn't her name, and Jack well knew it.

He thought it was funny and she thought it was annoying, but overall she was quite happy with him. He was a good provider, an excellent protector, and very attentive. She doubted if other raven cocks would fly to the very northern tip of Suffolk to look for her. He was very old, but he still managed to make fertile eggs every year, and they had raised many nests of healthy chicks. She liked it very much when he kissed her and so what more could a raven hen ask for?

But today she was not pleased with him. Not at all. He was insisting that they take over a raggedy old crow's nest he found high in a large tree on a busy road in the middle of a town. It was an absolutely inappropriate place to raise chicks. There were farmer fields just a few miles away. But no, he wanted this particular nest, and nothing else would do.

But he told her she was beautiful and promised solemnly that he would protect her and their chicks from the seagulls, and they would have frequent holidays to the Kent Downs. So with much grumbling and fluffing of feathers she agreed to make do with this totally inadequate nest. Just this one year though. Then she was heading back to the Kent Downs whether he followed or not.

Jack was happy with the nest and quickly made sure Jill was laying fertile eggs because once she laid her eggs she wasn't going anywhere. He was happy to sit on the eggs – much happier than usual because when he sat he could watch the front door of the lord's house. The lord and the elf didn't go in and out the front door very much, but that was probably because they ported whenever they left, leaving the front door to the Amazon guy and take-away deliveries.

He noticed the lights came on behind drawn drapes and he figured out that there was a bedroom on the first floor whose windows faced the street which was probably where the lord slept. He also noticed a little light coming from a cellar window at night. That would be where the elf slept.

He noted when they were there and when they were gone and he adapted his own foraging and incubating schedule to complement theirs.

A few days after the nest was established he was flying around the KFC hoping to scavenge some bits of chicken when he saw the lord leave a little shop, The Rum Lot, and then he knew where they went during the day.

Now it was just a matter of making sure this lord was sane. If she was okay, he'd fly in for a chat, but he wasn't going to risk his hen with their new eggs and his own safety by being too hasty. This was a delicate business.

_____

Caddy

Caddy didn't have a clue how she woke up Tony and was always rather embarrassed when she told him she was so stinking drunk she couldn't remember a thing. He didn't think anything of it because that's what lords did; they got drunk. The phrase "drunk as a lord" didn't port out of nowhere.

She didn't think it would do her any good to try getting drunk again because there was no assurance she would repeat whatever it was she did and Tony readily agreed. The last thing he wanted to deal with was an unpredictable drunken lord who didn't know what her abilities were.

She did know, from Tony's more sober memory, that she was singing and playing an instrument. That's what he heard that woke him up. She was calling for him to wake up and come to her, and since she was a lord, that's what he had to do. He answered her call.

So Caddy tried to recreate in her mind every aspect of that night to search for clues that would allow her to do it again.

She was on the shore when she sang, but that's not where Tony emerged. He emerged in Kensington Gardens and she made him take her to the exact spot. It showed no evidence that an elf had emerged there – no scars in the grass, no piles of dirt, no egg sac or shells or whatever it was he had to fight his way free from.

When he was free from the sac, naked, dripping with fluids, confused, and cold, he had taken a deep breath and ported to Safe Haven, where he was shocked to the core with what he found there. As soon as he gathered his wits, he ported back to Lowestoft to listen for elves. He heard no elves, but he did smell Caddy and made his way to her house, where his story with her started.

None of that contained any information that would do Caddy any good.

Caddy

Sarah Nutt was organising the spring liatris planting on the long bed in Kensington Gardens. The Friends of Kensington Gardens (FOKG) committee had decided last year that they needed more vertical height in late summer, and while planting bulbs in February was not the norm, this was an exception.

The day was cold and raw, and everyone was bundled up in heavy coats, hats, and boots and huddled in a corner of the gardens, looking for a place to shelter from the wind. In the back, looking like a geriatric yeti, was Ms Caddy.

Sarah hadn't seen Ms Caddy for years. Literally. She couldn't remember when she had last set eyes on her. Ms Caddy had stopped coming to the meetings, but she did donate a little bit to the garden club accounts, and she always bought something from the garden club's stall at the fetes.

Sarah called out to the old lady and waved. "Ms Caddy! It's good to see you! It's been a long time! Are you going to plant with us today?"

Ms Caddy gave a muffled yes and held up a trowel. Sarah was happy; one more set of hands to help meant they could all get home a bit faster. She gave Ms Caddy a section to plant and a handful of bulbs and let her get to it.

Caddy started digging. She didn't know what she was looking for, but this was the area where Tony emerged; she wondered if it was different somehow from her own garden just two blocks away.

It smelled good. That was a plus considering that just a few years before she was born it was a rubbish tip until a few Lowestoft great and the good decided to use the land as a public works project to employ WW1 veterans. Today she couldn't smell any ancient garbage. The dirt smelled good. Clean.

She popped in a bulb and moved over a bit and dug her trowel in again, humming to herself. She liked gardening, but she was just too old to do much any more. But today she felt energised. She popped in another bulb, made sure it was right side up, then pressed down the soil and moved over a bit. The dirt was exactly like her garden. She didn't see any difference, and she certainly didn't see any elves.

She plunged her trowel deep into the soft, sandy loam, humming, then singing to herself.

As far as I've heard, the fight's still on

The line's not cut, and the whale's not gone

The Wellerman makes his regular call

To encourage the captain, crew and all

Soon may the Wellerman come

To bring us sugar and tea and rum

One day, when the tonguing is done

We'll take our leave and go

There was some resistance, maybe a root, maybe an ancient bit of Jazz Age garbage, but she had to push hard and without realising until she did it, she pushed with her arms but also with that unknown muscle that made the baubles float and move.

The gardeners heard Ms Caddy scream and jump up like she had hit a live wire. Sarah dashed over right away. The last thing she needed was one of her pensioner volunteers to keel over in the middle of the Long Bed. That would be a health and safety issue and mean a lot of forms to fill out. Ms Caddy stood staring at the hole, holding the trowel like a sword, and was as pale as she could be with almost a greenish tint to her that was really alarming.

"Ms Caddy! Caddy! Are you all right? What's wrong? Do you need a doctor?"

Caddy turned to look at Sarah and gave her a weak smile. The colour returned to her cheeks.

"I'm so sorry to frighten you. I hit the most enormous worm, and it startled me."

Sarah laughed. "Well we do have some good sized earthworms here! As long as you're okay…"

"I'm fine, but thank goodness that was my last bulb. I think I'll go home now and have a cup of tea. I'm cold!"

"You do that, Ms Caddy. Thanks for coming!"

Caddy

Caddy burst into the sitting room where Tony was sitting at her big computer making improvements to her accounting program. He had hacked into the online applications master server and was adjusting some of the code to run a bit smoother and had removed a formatting glitch. He didn't think they'd mind.

"TONY!!" She ran up to the little man and jerked him right out of the chair and gave him a smothering bear hug. "TONY!!"

She danced around the room with him; she couldn't help herself. The energy had to go somewhere. "TONY!!!"

"Ms Caddy! I can't breathe!"

"Tony, I felt them! They're in the Gardens!" And she did her awkward jig again. The woman simply could not dance.

"I felt them. They're there! Elves, Tony! I felt elves!"

Then she threw herself on the sofa and looked at him, grinning.

"I guess I should take off my coat and boots."

Tony was stunned. He couldn't say anything at all.

"I'm going to calm down and rest and have a think. Unless I can think of a reason not to, I'm going out tonight and see if I can wake them up. "

"I'm going with you, Ms Caddy."
"Of course you are, Tony. I insist."

Caddy and Tony

She had a nap and then sat down to an enormous dinner with Tony. She wondered how her grocery bill was doing lately.

They debated the time to go to the gardens when it would be the most deserted. Caddy pointed out that parts of the garden had Council security cameras trained on it, and Tony looked thoughtful and wondered if he could hack the security system and turn it off while they were there.

"Probably not, Tony. You don't even know who's running the things, their ISP, or any address to get in, and I'm sure their master computers are pretty secure."

Tony shrugged.

"I'll try, Ms Caddy."

"I bet you can't, Tony."

And that's when she first learnt about elves and gambling. Elves love a good bet, not the random lotto types of gambling, but betting based on skill and challenges. Tony glowered.

"How much do you want to bet, Ms Caddy."

"Winner chooses the next take-away."

Done and they shook on it.

They decided on one in the morning. The pubs would be closed, the prom deserted, and they would have a couple of hours of dark to work in before the first early joggers were out and about.

Caddy would take her violin. The old acoustic guitar had been claimed by the sea, and the violin was smaller to carry anyway. It meant she couldn't sing and play at the same time, but she was hoping that it didn't matter what *made* the music. What mattered was her pushing the music and using it to command the elves to come to her. When she sang the old sea shanty, the elves weren't waking to the words but to her as a lord and her commands. The music was a way to focus, a scaffold for her magic that allowed her to reach the elves. That's what she felt anyway. She prayed she was right.

She hoped she was strong enough to get one to come up. From what she heard from Tony, as lord-power went she was pretty weak beer.

She laid down to get a few hours of sleep, but her mind was racing, and she didn't sleep as well as she wanted.

One o'clock came, and Tony ported next to her bed and shook Caddy awake.

"It's time, Ms Caddy."

She peed and put on a jumper because she knew
that she would have to take her coat off to play. It was still
bitterly cold out and the wind howled, but she couldn't play
a violin dressed up like an Eskimo, so she was just going to
have to risk the cold.

Tony was dressed for war. He wore black from top
to bottom and had one of Caddy's elf knives strapped to his
boot.

"You look like the accountant from hell, Mr Tony."

"I'm the accountant who has been to hell, Ms
Caddy." He looked grim. "Orcs still exist. I've seen them
here in Lowestoft. I'm prepared."

Caddy stopped smiling and nodded. This was
serious business.

"Port first if anything comes up. Don't fight. Port to
Safe Haven."

Tony agreed. That would be best.

They slipped out of the house and walked to the
park. Unknown to them they
were being followed.

At the park Caddy walked to the Long Bed where she had planted the bulbs. The earth was still disturbed by the gardener's work, but it was tidy. They might be volunteers, but they
were good gardeners.

She felt awkward and not a little silly. What would she say to anyone who came by and asked what an ancient woman was doing in the park at one in the morning? Playing her violin for the fairies? She would be put in a care home so fast Tony wouldn't have time to port her away.

Failure. That's what she was afraid of. Not care homes or orcs or anything else. Just failure.

All of her life there was someone standing next to her making sure she didn't get too good at what she was doing, making sure she didn't get a big head, pulling her back down to earth and telling her they were doing her a big favour. Every success she ever had was due to her fear of failure. She hated to fail because that meant all the whisperers were right.

She didn't know what to do and if she failed Tony they would both be miserable if for different reasons.

She took the violin out of the case. It was already in tune, but she tuned it again.

Mr Bunn once said, a thousand lives ago, that she could be a concert violinist if she wanted it badly enough. He was wrong, of course. Wanting is not enough. It never is.

But tonight she wanted.

Tonight she will play.

All evening, when she lay on her lumpy bed pretending to nap, she thought about what to play. She wanted to play something with a driving beat to wake the elves up. It needed to be yearning, commanding, rhythmic. Caddy didn't often write her own music; there were already plenty of wonderful pieces written by brilliant composers to use. It was more important to find the best song for her purpose than to show off her composing skills.

Tonight it was going to be Vivaldi. *La Folia* to start. That would be the wake-up song. *Four Seasons-Winter* to end, to drive them to the surface and to her.

That was the plan. She had no idea if it would work.

The little garden was quiet. The houses on the street were dark as their occupants dreamt of everything but the miracle that was happening on the other side of the garden gates.

She set her bow, drew out a long, clear note, and began to play.

She played, pushing the music to the elves with that part of her soul, that muscle she exercised when she moved the baubles, and the music was insistent, commanding.

The piece alternated between slow and fast, allowing the sleepers to rest as they journeyed towards her, but those respites ended, and she forced the elves to move, to obey.

Wake. It's time. Wake. Wake!

Her eyes glowed green, and sweat poured off her in great dripping sheets as her entire body focussed the energy she controlled into her waking song.

It's time! It's time to wake and come home to me. It's time for re-birth.

She stopped and lined to Tony and gave him the most beautiful, beatific smile. They were awake. She could feel them stirring. Her whole body began to glow green, and when she resumed playing it was Vivaldi's short, intense *Winter.*

Come to me. Come to me. Come to me. Come. *Come! Come!*

And then it was over.

The garden was absolutely silent. Even the sea, far down the cliff, was quiet.

They waited.

All Tony could hear was Caddy's rasping breath as she gulped air. She swayed a bit.

Then the ground around them erupted.

Elves exploded all around her, bursting from the ground in giant reptilian egg sacs.

Tony watched with horror and remembered his own struggle to free himself of the sac and how he felt like he was going to drown in the amniotic fluid that filled the space. He leapt forward with his elf knife and cut a slit, and out burst a perfect little form. A woman.

She was groggy, confused, and looked to Caddy who pointed to her and said, "Port! Port to Safe Haven!" And the woman saw the laser green eyes of a lord and did as she was told. She ported, leaving a gold shower of sparkling embers behind.

While that was happening Tony was running from sac to sac, cutting slits and pulling the elves out. He screamed to port as soon as he could get them to understand.

One tiny little boy ran naked and crying to Caddy, and she picked him up and threw him in the sky. "PORT!!" And suddenly a female elf ported from the sky, grabbed him, and together they ported away.

Someone was coming. A human. It was a bobby, walking up the Prom, looking for late night drunks who didn't make it home from last call at the pubs.

He saw the sparkling lights from the porting and started walking quickly to the seaside gate to the gardens. Ravers, he thought. Kids making late night mischief.

"Tony! Move them *OUT*!" Tony ran to the last two and slit their sacs and pulled the wet, squirming, birth-drunk elves out of their wet prisons, and the three of them all ported at the same time, leaving a bright shower of sparks.

All the elves were gone.

Caddy grabbed her violin and ran towards the street gate as fast as her ancient legs would carry her. The bobby turned the corner and yelled at her to stop. She looked back, and just as he stepped into the garden a great black bird flew into his face, and he had to duck and cover or he would have lost an eye. Caddy ran. The bobby ran. But he was a lot younger and much more fit, and he covered the ground quickly. She made it to the gate, and as she turned the corner Tony was there, and she ran into a porthole and disappeared.

The bobby turned the corner, and there was nothing there. No ravers. No kids. Nothing.

Tony ported her back to her sitting room, and before she could even turn, he was gone.

Caddy sat there in the dark not daring to believe what had happened. Then the shock of disbelief turned into a wild cry of triumph and victory, and she jumped up and down in her unlit sitting room and screamed with joy.

Jack

Like most birds (except owls and everyone knew how crazy those fuckers are) Jack didn't like flying at night. It was dangerous. But when he saw the lord and the elf *walk* to the garden at one in the morning, not port, he knew something was up.

Jack watched the entire performance.

The lord was powerful. She was an elemental, he could see that right away. She did many things wrong and diffused a lot of energy which wasted her power and tired her out, but that was because she was obviously untaught. She probably had to learn everything herself. Jack was sure the elf who lived with her, as clever as elves can be, didn't know how to tutor a lord.

She woke up elves. The one who lived with her was one, but Jack didn't know how many others she had woken up and were living further afield. He didn't know how long she had been doing this work, but from tonight's performance she was successful at it.

She was waking up elves! Good for her!

If Jack had been born a songbird he would have broken out in song.

_____

Caddy

Caddy did nothing but eat and sleep for two days. The first day Tony didn't show up at all, and Caddy was sure he was with the newly re-birthed elves. Goodness knows what they were talking about, but she was very happy they were together. It would take years to fully adjust to this new world, so they would need each other to lean on.

The second day she found food on the table in the kitchen just like when Tony first appeared. That was nice but not really necessary. Despite her dotage she still remembered how to operate a can opener and if need be there was always take-away.

Once she recovered from the initial exhaustion she felt great. Her back was straightening up, and, gods help her, she was getting boobs back again. She started to look a bit more like she felt she should look. She wasn't forty again, not by a long shot. She didn't even look sixty, but when you're well over a hundred looking and feeling like you're seventy is not a bad thing.

But the very best part was that her little finger was almost totally straight now, and she could really play the little Spanish guitar the way it should be played. She started to seriously think about getting a new acoustic to replace the one claimed by the sea.

The third day she got up early with the intention of going to the shop. She didn't know she would close the shop for a couple of days because she didn't anticipate how exhausting it would be to wake the elves. At this point Caddy didn't understand how much of her abilities she was using because as she played the magic was just a part of her music, so she didn't understand how much energy was passing through her body. Like an elite athlete, she had a lot of natural ability, but she still had a long way to go to build up her strength to use that ability to its full potential.

When she walked into the kitchen for breakfast it was packed to overflowing with elves. Including Tony there were twelve of them. Some were sitting at the table, others sitting on the countertops, others bustling around trying to work and clean while the others just got in the way. They were all properly dressed with not a toga in sight. They chattered and laughed and made a huge noise until Caddy walked in and then it was like a radio switched off. They all turned to her, their eyes huge and mostly worried.

Caddy remembered Tony's initial reaction to her. She was frightening, but she had also been a teacher for forty years, and she knew how to walk into a room and take control of it. These weren't kids, but they were adults who had been through hell and back. Just like children they needed reassurance. They needed to know where they stood with her.

Caddy waited in the doorway and let them have a good look at her. When they were all paying attention she posed in the namaste position, hands with palms together, and gave them a low bow. When she got back up she smiled and said, "Welcome to my house. My home is your home for as long as you need it."

There was a collective gasp. A lord had bowed – and bowed first – to an elf!

Tony grinned and stood up and returned the bow. "Good morning, Ms Caddy! Thank you for helping us."

Then the elves looked at each other and turned as one to Caddy and copied Tony exactly. "Good morning, Ms Caddy! Thank you for helping us."

Caddy smiled back. At least she didn't get the mooning backwards bow. Tony had been talking to them.

"You're most welcome. I am always here to help you, just as you are here to help me. We need each other, and later we will have many things to talk about as you begin to live in this new world.

"But first things first, is there any porridge for breakfast? I'm starved."

Caddy

While Tony didn't know how to wake up elves, one of the group did, and without mentioning it to Caddy (why would a lord be interested in that?), they organised themselves into little work groups.

Tony and Norma were to work at the shop, the three who knew what they were doing were to work at waking elves, and the housekeeping and lord maintenance duties would be rotated among the rest. They could only wake up one or two a day, but these elves were their clan and they worked every day without rest.

Caddy thought about it and told them she would play once a week for them because she would need a couple days rest afterwards, and she didn't want to burn out or get sick. If she could waken ten or so in one go, and they woke up one a day, that meant by the end of the month they would have seventy elves. And that was the start of a village.

The next biggest issue was where were they all to live? At the moment they all seemed to be camping out either in the cellar with Tony or spending the night in the depressing Safe Haven. They wanted and needed houses in the Lowestoft area soil.

Lowestoft is a market town of about 72,000, so a good number of people, but they were all arranged in a line along the seashore making the town very long and very narrow. It was bordered on the west with fens and farmland, and just a bit to the north was the vast inland swamp called the Norfolk Broads.

Caddy called a meeting and the 13 of them – only now it was 17 – sat in her sitting room and she asked them what they wanted to do.

Vernon was an old, grizzled elf and seemed to be a clan leader. He spoke for them.

"We want to build houses, Ms Caddy, and there is some good land just north of town near Somerleyton. We've decided to go there."

Caddy tilted her head.

"Have you paid for it yet Vernon?"

"Paid? Who pays for land?" Vernon was confused. How can anyone *own* land?

Caddy nodded. She had had an inkling this was going to happen. She had been listening to them talk. Her Elvish was very good now.

"Everybody – you need to listen to me and think hard on what I'm going to say. You have been asleep for 3,500 years. In those years humans and orcs have lived here and had a lot of wars and a lot of arguments over things like land. They have come up with a system where people own bits of land. They buy and sell it. If you build on their land that is stealing from them just as if I walked into your house and kicked you out of your bed and slept in it."

"But Ms Caddy, you're a lord. You can do that." They all nodded.

"Okay. Let me start again. Things have changed in 3,500 years, and right now we won't have humans and orcs attacking us because they have forgotten all about us. But if you go taking what they think is their land they'll get testy, and we don't want that. You are only 17 in number –"

"Eighteen." Tony looked at his phone, he was sure his roster was up to date.

" – and there are three *billion* of them. You have to operate under their rules. This is what I want you to do. I want you to look for land for sale and buy it. I have money in the bank. I hope I have enough, but if I don't I'll go take a loan out or something. If you see a bit of unused land you want to buy, then make the owner an offer. But do *not* just go start building. That will cause a lot of problems."

She turned to Tony.

"Tony, how much do I have in my savings account now?" Tony looked at his tablet and then said, "Pounds sterling? Eighteen million, five hundred sixty three thousand, two hundred sixty-three. And sixteen pence."

Caddy blinked.

"There is no way that's right."

Tony was offended and then blushed. "I'm sorry Ms Caddy, it's eighteen pence. I misread it. Apologies."

Caddy spoke slowly. She didn't want to embarrass the elf.

"Tony, that's a bit more than I expected. Can you tell me where the additional funds came from?"

"Rounding errors, Ms Caddy." Tony saw her obvious confusion and then started to explain about bank and large corporation accounting methods and rounding errors, and immediately he lost the room. Elves started to chat with each other, some pulled out tablets, and two left the meeting entirely.

"Be quiet, please! Tony, please start again. Only the short stupid people version. For me."

"Ms Caddy, every large accounting department, every bank, every government entity that handles invoices and payments in the human world loses money. Not as in bad investments, but as in "physically loses track of it". They change accounting programs and not everything transfers properly. A file goes inactive and the money inside it is lost. Transactions are divided and a penny is left over." Tony's voice lowered as if he were talking about an obscenity. "*And they just write it off.* They don't even look for it. They just write. It. Off.

So I developed a little AI program that hacks into accounts, looks for errors and lost accounts, and fixes them. It straightens up their books for them.

I made the program replicate itself and look for new companies and entities, so it's all automatic now." Tony gave Caddy a smile. A very self-satisfied one.

Caddy's mouth made a little O. The penny dropped. Literally. "So when the accounts are fixed and balanced what happens to the odd pence you end up with? Is it in my savings account now?"

"Of course it is, Ms Caddy. They probably paid less than a pound for a bit of forensic accounting maintenance that would have cost them thousands of pounds. I've seen the accounting bills! It's a bargain!"

"How much is coming in Tony?"

Tony considered and looked at his tablet again.

"It took a while to build up because it's a geometric progression and started at one pence, but it's about a million a day now. There was a big jump last week when the program crossed over to France. I expect a huge leap when it hits the US. They're very sloppy."

Caddy thought about it. There were ethical issues with breaking into people's computer systems, but on the other hand, the elves did deserve compensation for what humans had done to them. And at a penny here and a penny there, it didn't seem to be causing them any harm.

"Okay, then. I guess we'll have enough money to do what we want to in the human world!"

Caddy nodded to Vernon.

"Vernon, just make sure everything is done legally according to His Majesty's government, and I'm happy. We pay for everything, and we trade fairly, and we DON'T give humans any reason to go crazy on elves. Understood?" Caddy looked around. "Does everyone understand that?"

"Yes, Ms Caddy!" they all said in unison.

And the next day the elves went on a land and building buying spree.

Caddy and the Elves

It was very, very early in the morning, and Caddy, Vernon, Norma, and Tony were walking around Fen Park getting soaked in the dewy grass. Fen Park was a little neighbourhood park just four or five blocks west of Caddy's house and the secluded wild spaces in it were not used much at all.

Caddy was listening for hibernating elves and she hoped that this little park would be a good spot to try. Vernon had said that if any were buried under nearby houses and roads they would come up diagonally. Instinctively they would try to find the easiest route, and an open space like a park was much better than having them pop up in people's back gardens. That would be a nightmare.

"Can you hear them Vernon? I can, just a little. There seems to be a group over here by the children's swings. "

"I don't hear them like you do. Ms Caddy. I feel vibrations."

She sighed. "This is hard. You would think in 3,500 years there would be some lords running around with experience at this."

A voice in the trees said, "Lords are very, very rare."

They all looked up, but they couldn't see who was talking. The only living thing they saw was a big black bird. A raven.

Jack turned his good eye to Caddy and bowed.

"Jack One-Eye, at your service, Madam."

"Oh! Hello!" Caddy looked over at Tony, but he was gone. All the elves had disappeared as soon as they heard Jack talk. Caddy didn't even hear them port away.

She looked back at the raven.

"Cadence Aeldor, sir. I'm pleased to meet you." She held out her hands and smiled. "It seems my friends have other things to do."

"I scared them. They'll be back. I hope without bows and arrows."

"Are you a danger to me?"

"No, Lord Cadence. I mean you no harm, to be sure, I wish you every success." Jack gave a little hop. "I think it's wonderful that you are bringing the elves back!"

"If I'm safe around you then you have nothing to fear from the elves. May I call you Jack?"

He bounced, and Caddy took that as a nod.

"Then you may call me Ms Caddy. So, Jack, what do you know about elves that makes you happy they are back?"

"Balance, Ms Caddy, balance. This world is unbalanced. You have taken an important but fragile step towards righting the world."

He looked at the old woman. She was very ill. If she was a healthy lord she wouldn't look so old. Age happens when the body starts to fail. A lord in their prime, when they are the most healthy and strong, looked like they were neither young nor old. They look like they are about 30 or 40, 45 at most. This woman looked twice that.

She was too ill to be alone and the elves needed to come back and tend to her.

"Be careful, Ms Caddy. There are forces out there that don't want elves to come back. And they will do anything – anything – to stop that. They are slow, and they have become lazy and complacent, but sooner or later they will come for you and the elves."

Caddy listened.

"So there is a reason the elves haven't come back for 3,500 years. Is it because there were no lords to call them?"

"Oh, there were lords, Ms Caddy, but they were killed before they found their powers, and they were murdered while they were weak. You, by some miracle, have made it to adulthood. You have slipped under their radar, and in the meantime you have found your ability. That makes you dangerous. When they find out about you they will come for you. If you die, so will the elves."

"And are you going to tell these enemies I'm here, Jack?"

Jack laughed. She had no idea.

"Oh, Ms Caddy, fuck no. There is not much a ridiculous bird like myself can do, but I'm on your side. Good luck and be careful!"

And he flew off. The elves were back and waiting for him to leave, and
she needed them there.

Caddy watched him leave and stood staring at the empty space for a long time, thinking.

Caddy

"It's not –" Caddy said between bites of her fish and chips, " – that I am weirded out for having a conversation with a crow –"

"Raven, Ms Caddy."

" – but it's what he said that bothers me."

Tony nodded. Tony, the formidably efficient Norma, and the two elves on today's housekeeping rotation (Lillibet and George) were having a dinner of fish and chips from Gibbs Chippy.

"When someone goes out of their way to warn you of danger you can agree or disagree, but you can't ignore the warning. He obviously believed it was important to say something. He didn't have to."

"What if he is lying and really working for 'they,' whoever 'they' are?" said Lillibet.

"If 'they' want to kill me and keep you guys in hibernation, then why warn me? Just do it. It would be easier," Caddy answered.

George suddenly stood up and coughed. They all looked at him.

"I think we need more vinegar." And he ran off.

"I don't think more vinegar will keep the evil forces at bay." Caddy smiled.

"Oh, that's silly." Norma didn't get the joke.

"Not any sillier than having existential conversations with ravens," said Tony.

Caddy ate her last chip and looked sorrowfully at her plate. Tony and Lillibet both slid their plates away from the lord. So she ate one of George's.

"I think," said Caddy, "the best thing for me to do is to wake up as many elves around here as possible. And we need to get the humans around here on our side."

She looked at Tony. "Tony, I want you to hire Ellen away from the council. You and Norma go and talk to her. Pay her whatever she needs and then double it. She is very, very loyal to me and didn't freak out when she met you. She knows how people think, and her experience with humans will guide us."

"But she's a *human*, Ms Caddy!"

"That's the point, Tony. That's the point."

Caddy

The next night they gathered in Fen Park. There were twenty-two elves in Lowestoft now, and Caddy didn't know half of them, but they all knew what to do. About ten of the elves walked with Caddy, and the rest made a circle around the park to guard it and prevent accidental intruders.

A couple were soldier elves, battle-scarred veterans with sad eyes that turned cold when they took up positions at the park gates. No bobbies would make it past them. Caddy had to tell them quite severely that, no, they could not kill anyone who wandered by. No, not even if they were orcs just passing through. Only if their lives were at stake. Every intruder must be ported someplace neutral, like on the other side of the bridge at the north end of town. They grumbled, but orders were orders and they wouldn't disobey their Lord.

Each one had their own elf knife and were dressed in black. Caddy thought it was like having a pack of really small ninjas around her. She was afraid of not seeing them in the dark and tripping over them, but they were careful to stay out from under her feet.

Caddy knew what to expect now. She walked around the park, occasionally stopping and listening, and Vernon thought of foxes hunting for mice in the fields. Only this fox had green glowing eyes. When she found a spot that met some mysterious Caddy criteria, she unpacked her violin and placed it under her chin, set the bow, and looked to Vernon. He nodded; they were ready.

And she played.

It was a different song this time; this was a different place, but the theme was the same. A waking song to get the attention of the sleeping elves, then a pause, and then a commanding calling song to get them to come to her.

It was still very hard and very exhausting, but this time she knew what to expect and she knew what to *feel* for. So her force, her pull, her whatever-it-was that made that ability muscle work, worked a little better and was a little more focussed.

She pulled up as many as she could and worked her music as hard as she was able, and in the end Caddy felt that few were left behind. But Vernon had told her earlier that if she said some were still in hibernation down there the elves would go in themselves and rescue the laggards one by one. No one would be abandoned to forever sleep.

Caddy drew out the last eerie note, and her part of the re-birth was done. And like the first time, she was totally spent, soaked with sweat, and dizzy from the insulin crash that comes from using every last bit of energy in her body. Under her feet, the soft boggy earth of Fen Park jiggled like unset custard.

Then the ground exploded, and out shot fifteen or more huge, rubbery egg-like sacs, each one filled with an elf. The reborn elves ran up to the sacs, slit open a hole to release the unborn elf inside, and immediately lifted dripping, squirming elves off the ground. Freed of their ties to Mother Earth, they immediately ported with a shower of golden sparks to Safe Haven.

As fast as it started it was over. One minute was music, then birthing chaos, then silence. An elf came up to Caddy – she didn't know who – and, without touching her because her green glowing body would burn them, pointed to a port hole, and she stepped through it and was in her sitting room.

She was alone. The elves had other things to do just then, so she sat on her sofa and shuddered and trembled as her body fought with exhaustion and the battling surge of hormones in her system reset. But, oh, it felt good.

Caddy

Norma popped in to make sure that the housekeeping elves showed up and to report to Caddy that thirty were reborn out of Fen Park. And this morning they went in and one-by-one pulled up five more. A good night's work!

Caddy was happy, the elves were ecstatic, and a mass of elves bustled around her kitchen chirping and trilling with the news of who had woken up, who they were related to, what news they had of what they were now calling Before Times. There was a constant train of elves popping in and out of the kitchen to pass on their own news, to thank Caddy personally, or to hear the latest gossip.

Some of the news was sad as confirmation of deaths came out, but tearful, joyous reunions balanced that out. Sadness that a loved one was not in this group was balanced with the hope that they were still asleep and still might be found. Every reunion reinforced their determination to find more of their friends, lovers, and family.

There were twenty-four reborn elves when Caddy went to Fen Park. The next morning there were fifty-nine, and with most of those elves searching for and waking one a day, Caddy could see the local elf population exploding to a thousand by the end of the month even if she did nothing at all.

In the meantime she ate an enormous breakfast and then went back to bed and slept for a day and a half. They would just have to deal with whatever came up without her.

Ellen

Every time Ellen sat in her new office, she was a bit stunned at life's turn of events. She now worked for RumLot, Ltd. as Vice President for Human and Elf Relations, Public Relations, and Government Liaison. Her new office was gorgeous, precisely to her taste with light woods, oriental carpets, and pretty feminine touches in the soft furnishings. She was making stupid money. Tony told her to name her price, and she threw out a number she knew he would never agree to, but, to her horror, he did. And then when she agreed to leave ESC, he doubled it.

She had a personal elf assigned to her to port her to wherever she needed to go in town.

A personal elf.

When she had to go further afield she had a company car. A really nice one.

She really had no idea what she was supposed to do to earn all this, but after a couple of days she discovered she would be earning her penny. There were constant issues that popped up and she was the person who negotiated between elves and the modern world. Questions that needed answering like – why do elves need planning permission to build a house? How does an elf pay council tax? Who does a solicitor contact when their human client needs to talk to an elf and do elves sign contracts? Do elves need a driver's licence? What to do about rumours and reports of elves on Facebook?

All of those things needed to be dealt with and soon Ellen was swamped with tasks to manage, position papers to write guiding elf/human contacts, and phone calls to make. It was a challenging job, but she was having the time of her life.

And she loved the elves, every one of them. Norma, for instance, was a hoot. She was a little under a metre tall, looked, acted, and dressed like a 1940s Rosalind Russell in *His Girl Friday*. She wasn't a star reporter, but she was a formidable personal assistant to Ms Caddy and did a huge amount of work in the shop as well as in the back office where managing the integration of elves into the modern world was really taking place.

Caddy came into the shop less often now. She seemed to spend all of her time eating, sleeping, practising her music, and generally being the leader of the elves, and she gave all appearances to be happy with that. Ellen had never seen Caddy do anything overtly magical, but Ellen could now see that magic had floated around Caddy for years. That door thing, for instance. That wasn't normal.

The elves called her 'the lord" when Caddy wasn't around and Ms Caddy when she was. Ellen didn't know what a lord was in elf-world, but she was getting an idea. A lord certainly wasn't a deity, but there was definitely more to the title than a human's earl or prince. The older ones were very grateful that their lord was Ms Caddy. One told her they had worked with a lot worse. A lot of them were assholes.

Neptune

Thirty-five hundred years ago, Neptune was playing on the other side of the world with his merfolk clan when Gaia made her final, drama-queen, selfish, insanely stupid exit. As a leader and keeper of balance, he had always been neutral about Gaia, and although he thought her a bit wishy-washy and prissy for his taste, all-in-all he didn't have strong feelings about her one way or the other. He lived in the sea and she was almost entirely on land, and what she did there was her business.

Until the minute her business affected him and his merfolk. Then he cared deeply.

The death of the Elemental and Realm Lords, the rebellion of the orcs and humans, and their relentless extermination of the weaker lords and elves was a profound shock to his merfolk. Merfolk had a great deal of commerce with elves, their distant cousins, and while there were many physical, mental, and ability differences that had developed over the millennia to cope with their different environments, they were still the same people in many ways.

Neptune didn't like what humans and orcs were doing, but it wasn't his business, so he didn't do anything other than gamble, drink, and play with the mer-ladies just as he always had. His not-my-problem-attitude was, he realised later, a profound dereliction of duty.

The slaughter of the elves terrified the merfolk, and they feared for their own lives. When elves went into hibernation and left the physical world, the merfolk did, too.

One day they were there, and the next day they were gone. All they left was a note for Neptune that said, "Wake us up when everything is back to normal. Love you lots, xxxooo."

Neptune didn't know what to do. He didn't know how to wake up his people. He needed his merfolk in order to be healthy himself. And while that was a practical issue, he also needed them to love. At first he was furious at them for just dumping him and leaving without warning, but then he grieved, and as he grieved he realised he had done nothing to make them feel secure in his leadership.

The land lords had not protected their elves; what made them think a single lord like Neptune could protect all of the merfolk of the seven seas? He had been arrogant and cocksure for thinking his kindness to them was enough to keep them bound to him in tough times. By ignoring the slaughter on land he certainly wasn't working for Balance. He had never told his people he could and would take care of them. He never told a single merfolk he loved them.

He was a party boy, a fun guy. He had given them no reason to think he was dependable when life took a rocky turn and it took centuries for him to come to terms with that.

So they did the only thing they knew to do to protect themselves and their children. Should they have talked this decision over with Neptune? No, why should they? He never showed concern over their lives and he often left without a word. So that's what they did.

He was profoundly lonely.

For decades he wandered the seas looking for a clue about how to wake them up, but there was nothing. Eventually, he gave up and sank into a deep depression mentally and physically. He sank to the very bottom of the deepest, coldest sea, and there he stayed.

Every five hundred years, give or take, he would shake off the lethargy, rise to the sunlight, and feed his skeletal body, practise his abilities, and get healthy again – just enough to take measure of the world and see if he should look for his merfolk again.

But he heard and saw nothing. Not a mermaid, not an elf, not a lord – nothing but humans and their stinking orcs. Every time he rose back up to the surface he would look far and wide, but after each discouraging scan of his realm, he would sink back into the deep to pass the vast time and to mourn the past and hope for a better future. Most of the time he just slept.

Nothing had ever disturbed his watery sleep. Until now.

A song had woken him up. Someone had called him. *Come to me, come to me.*

It was a woman; he knew that from the voice. At least it seemed female. He had been fooled before by female lords who took the form of men and male lords who took the form of women, but he was fairly sure this was a female. Not that it mattered. If this unknown lord of unknown gender was up for a little fun, so was Neptune.

But it wasn't sex that Neptune was looking for; that would come later if it was meant to be. What he wanted to know was that he was not alone.

He rose from the black depths and took measure of the world as it was now, and he was not pleased at all.

Neptune

The water was bitter cold, but Neptune didn't mind. He liked the tropics much better, where the warm water was clean and clear, but it wasn't the cold that bothered him here; it was the stink. It just wasn't very nice water to breathe in, not with all the boats with their diesel and leaky bilge and sludge tanks.

He broke the surface just far enough out to take a look at the shore. It was high tide and he sprawled out on a sandbar. The waves crashing over it buffeted him, but he was Neptune, and a few little whitecaps that would keel over a boat meant nothing to him.

There was a wide sandy beach, and above the beach were rows of human houses. He passed many of their buildings as he swam near the shore and from what he could see there were humans everywhere. They were like a plague of jellyfish. There didn't seem to be any place they couldn't build on and foul the shore with their strange homes.

Neptune liked the sandbar because he knew the boats wouldn't bother him there. For human sailors this was shallow, treacherous water and they avoided the shoals. Not that humans couldn't afford to lose one or two. There were untold numbers of their blasted floating things! There were tiny ones that fit only one man to huge floating islands of steel. Whatever humans had been doing on land the last five-hundred years he was asleep he didn't know, but they had certainly spent a good deal of time building stinking, dirty, *noisy* ships.

Oh ye gods – the noise! Pings and booms and whines and creaks. He could hardly hear himself think, and he could see it was driving the whales crazy. One of the human's undersea ships boomed at him as he was swimming by and he thought he was going to go deaf. It made him so mad he punched a hole in the side of the thing and the implosion from the water pressure made it crumple like a piece of rotten tube coral.

It sank to the bottom, and he could hear the screams of the humans and orcs inside as they drowned, which didn't bother him a bit. After a few minutes there was blessed silence and he swam on.

Neptune sat on the sand bar regularly now. He had heard the songs twice, and he was getting closer to the lord who was making them. Her first song was for the sea (as it should be, he thought) and once the music woke him he knew what to listen for. Her music was clearer and stronger but not just because he was in her waters. She was stronger, too. He could tell.

She would make music again and he would track it down; he just had to be patient. When he did she would be on land and he would have to change to a human form to go find her, and he was not looking forward to that, not one bit. So he waited in the shallows and watched the beach and listened for music. He was not as healthy as he should be, and changing was going to be extremely painful. But it would be a very small price to pay to talk to a lord once again.

Then, one morning, he saw one. An elf. It was a mother and a child strolling along the firm wet sand where the waves met the shore, the hyper-vigilant mother holding the child's hand while it played.

Neptune cried. He never told anyone the emotions he felt when he watched that most ordinary of scenes because words could never give it justice, but to see an elf! Oh, what a miracle! That elf mother walking on the shore meant the elves were waking up. Could that mean his mermaids and mermen are waking up, too?

Neptune understood then what was going on. The songs weren't for him; they were for the elves. She was calling the elves back to earth.

He sank back into the sea and cried salty tears of relief and hope. He didn't try to call to the tiny woman. Yelling at the elf would terrify her, and she would port her child away instantly, and for all he knew that might scare off the lord, too. Goodness knows what she had gone through in the last thirty-five hundred years!

Empathy had never been Neptune's strength, but he had learned a lot sleeping in his deep sea fissure. He had to be patient. He had to think about this woman lord and what she needed from him. This first meeting had to go perfectly, and he only had one chance to get it right. For the first time in his long, long, long life he was nervous about meeting a woman.

Wendell Bunn

The entire Lowestoft elf clan, more than one hundred strong now, was having a meeting in the back offices, and Caddy offered to watch the shop for an hour while they hashed out the next place to visit to wake up elves.

Should they stick close to home and go someplace like Normanston Park on the other side of Lake Lothing? Or should they stretch and go further out but still in a comfortable range like Great Yarmouth or Laxfield? Caddy's opinion was that they should go further out and use her ability to wake up bunches of elves. Then they could fill in between themselves with the increased manpower. That would grow the elf community much faster and more efficiently than using her once a week to plough over previously searched ground. It didn't matter to her where they started because eventually she would be doing both, but it mattered to them, so she let them hash it out. Once they decided on a direction she would work with the clan leaders to figure out the best exact location.

The bell softly jingled and dozing Caddy woke with a start. It only took the briefest of glances, but she knew this young man didn't have a penny to his name. No sales here. Tall, gawky, shouldering the inevitable heavy backpack (what on earth did they carry in those things?), he was dressed well-enough but was only one day away from desperately needing a shower. He wore boots. Not the working or hiking kind but old-fashioned knee boots. Cheap ones.

Stiff-backed, he worked his way around the shop, intently examining each rack as if the bauble of his dreams hid in there. He stroked his chin, thoughtfully scratching at the boy-stubble. He peered. He touched nothing and slowly made his way to the counter.

Caddy patiently eased up in her chair and waited. It would come. He wanted something.

"That elf in the window –"

Today Gertrude the Mannequin was dressed in her mermaid uniform with blue hair, seahorse jewellery, and mermaid tail, but Caddy wasn't going to argue with him about the sartorial differences between elves and mermaids. She nodded helpfully.

"Those pointed ears on her, do you have any more for sale?" He took a step towards the door, ready to bolt, but when Caddy shook her head and smiled he changed his mind.

"No, sir, those are shop display. You can buy them on Ebay very cheap." But of course, he knew that. The follow up question flew out of her mouth before she could help herself and she regretted it immediately.

"Is there anything else I can help you with? I see you like elves."

That was all the opening he needed, and the words fizzed out like a shook up bottle of cherry coke. She knew exactly what he was going to say before he said it.

He was a cos-player. He was into fantasy role-playing games. His persona was a goblin who "are not as mean as people think; they're just cheeky" and of course he didn't have a penny on him but thought the shop was really interesting and he would be back, and what was her opinion of gnomes?

His name was Wendell, and he offered his hand. So of course Caddy rather reluctantly shook it; it would have been rude to do otherwise. It was damp. Wendell was thrilled that Caddy hadn't thrown him out on his ear and by some miracle would chat for a few minutes about goblins (Caddy said she had no experience with goblins and Wendell gracefully accepted that), but soon she was bored with the (very very detailed, very very one-way) conversation about goblins, gnomes, and other non-human Dungeons & Dragons creatures. After a few long minutes of silence Wendell eventually twigged it was time for him to go.

"I'm off now, but I'll bring back my mum; she'll love this shop. And some money. I'm a bit short now."

Caddy nodded and leaned back in her chair, settling into pre-snooze mode. She didn't say a word but smiled and waved.

"I'll be back!"

Nodding again Caddy was sure he would be. If he could find the place.

But a half hour later Wendell did find the door to The Rum Lot. He trotted back with a Magic - The Gathering game card, the goblin one. This, he said, was what he was going for. What did she think? Could he look like a real goblin? Goblins weren't all bad, just mischievous.

Caddy looked at the card and didn't think the green, axe-wielding monster looked mischievous – he looked vicious – and she passed back the card and said gently, "Goblins don't exist. So I can't say if you could look like a real one. I guess you can dress up like this card and paint yourself green, but why? Why pretend you're a monster?"

He frowned. "Not many people play goblins. They're different from the usual elves and fairies and wizards. Besides, how do you know they don't exist? Can you say elves and fairies don't exist? You can't prove a negative."

Caddy leaned back in the office chair, smiling broadly, and her eyes glittered, but he didn't notice. He was frowning at the card.

"No, you can't prove a negative. In this huge world many things exist that we don't believe. The Queen in *Alice in Wonderland* said she believed in six impossible things before breakfast, which is silly and gullible, but she was telling Alice to stretch her mind and not be rigid. I believe in many things people think are impossible, but they're not impossible to me. I *do* try to keep an open mind, but," Caddy leaned forward, "goblins don't exist. Other bad things do but not goblins. Align yourself with the good guys, Wendell. You'll be happier for it."

Wendell looked at the old woman sitting on the chair in her jeans and Rum Lot t-shirt. She looked absolutely ordinary. She looked like his teachers at school, but she was talking with him about his passion for alternative worlds and almost no one but his gaming group did.

Suddenly he grinned.

"Okay, I'll find a good guy. Maybe a ranger. Or maybe an elf."

"You're too tall to be an elf, dear. Trust me."

At that point Tony ported in with Charlene who was taking over the desk.

"Ms Caddy, would you come to the meeting for a minute?"

She nodded and got up, winked at Wendell, and ported away.

Charlene climbed up to Caddy's chair, kneeled on the chair's seat, and leaned on the desk. She was very cute with her pointy ears, heavy dark blue plaits, and dirndl. Customers loved her.

"Can I help you, sir?"

Caddy

The decision was made to go north to Great Yarmouth and not use Caddy to move incrementally up through the north side of Lowestoft. They would go to Burgh Castle where the walls of ancient Roman ruins sit in a small park in the middle of marshy fields. It looked pretty isolated.

A few of the clan leaders and two soldiers would port out there that afternoon just to check it out, and if they thought it was safe then Caddy would go tomorrow morning and have a good walk around. A couple back-up locations were considered.

Caddy was happy with the plan and wasn't too worried about whether or not it was isolated enough. They had had two successful sessions in the middle of Lowestoft for heaven's sake! The only interruption was a lone bobby. She didn't think anyone would be around Burgh Castle at one in the morning, but in any case, the soldiers would be there.

When she walked around Burgh Castle she felt the hibernating elves stirring. There were many sleeping bodies down there; she could feel it. Caddy didn't have to think twice. She grinned at Vernon and the rest of the leaders and said, "Are you up for a little party tonight?" And they grinned back and ported back home in a flurry of snaps because there was a lot to do to get everyone ready.

Orcs

Jared was happy with his bro'. The boy had scored some good stuff and had found out where they could get a lot more. The brothers, and there were three of them, made a nice little living running a county line drug courier business, but this was a stash stolen from a rival so it was free stuff.

They could sit around, get fekkin' high, and not have to pay it back to anyone. How fekkin' good was that!

"Are you up for a little party tonight?" And of course they were. Who wouldn't be?

But they weren't going to share. No way. They lived in a house with a bunch of selfish fuckers who'd crash the party, and the boys knew from sad experience that once one of their flatmates found out half the neighbourhood would drop in, and the party would end up being a riot, and they'd get nothing.

So they'd buy some sausages, a couple bottles of something cheap from the off-licence, and have a little picnic with their well-earned booty.

Jared

Jared woke up. He lay flat on his back in a marshy area near the River Waveney, and how he got there he didn't know. He and the boys hadn't bothered with making a fire for the sausages but got down to business as soon as they got to the river bank. He could vaguely remember whooping and hollering and Davy running up the river path, but he had no idea where he was now. He grinned. That must have been some wild stuff.

He looked around. It was pitch dark, and heavy clouds meant that there wasn't even starlight to see by. Near him lay two lumps, and with a bit of kicking they moved. His brothers.

"Get the fuck up! You arseholes! Where the feck are we?"

They moaned, and he had to kick them again. Hard. Useless sods.

He didn't know where the path was, but it seemed he had a river to his right,
so the path must be –

"Bloody 'ell –" There were sparks of light and it wasn't far. A rave! Just the thing to go to. He kicked whoever was closer – Davy? – and pointed.

"Lookee here. We got a party to visit, bros!" And that got the boys up right quick. Jared told them to shut up.

"We need to sneak up just to see what's goin' on. You two go that way, and I'll go this way. I don't wanna run into coppers or nuth'n."

And that's what they did. Quietly, quietly they crept up from two different directions. In the space of a minute, Jared couldn't see them any more, and he was on his own. The soft damp ground made him silent. He made it to a little copse of trees that gave him some cover and stopped for a good look.

It was fekkin fairies! Little people! Fekkin fairies! Bloody 'ell.

He blinked. Maybe he was still high. That was some really really good stuff.

There were hundreds of them, and they were pulling eggs from the ground. Easter eggs! Some were nekkid and some were dressed, and the dressed ones would grab a nekkid one, and they would pop away in a shower of embers, and that is what he saw sparkling in the sky.

They must've been having a picnic because he could smell something really good, and it made his mouth water. Damn, he was hungry.

There was a scream to his right, and he could see his two damn fool brothers running like idiots right into the party. Shit. They were laughing and whooping and –

Then they were gone. Just like that. Poof. Gone.

The fairies were like ants in a kicked nest. They grabbed every egg, open or not, and within seconds they were gone, too.

No! They were – NO. NO!! They were *not* going to leave just like that. And he ran towards the rave. Then he saw her.

One of the fairies, a tiny girl, was havin' trouble getting a nekkid one out of the egg. She wasn't paying any attention to anything else and he saw his chance.

Three steps. That's all he needed.

She freed a nekkid man and threw him in the air, and he disappeared in a shower of sparks. At that exact minute Jared leapt out and grabbed her by the hair. And shit! did she scream! She struggled to free herself, but he grabbed her neck now and held her by the scruff of her neck. He shook her and laughed. She tried to slash at him with her tiny knife, but she was too small and didn't have the reach. It was really funny, watching her struggle, and he shook her again.

Then the oddest thing happened. He wondered what she would taste like, and once that thought got into his head he couldn't get rid of it. She's a fairy; she probably tastes like candy. He lifted her up, opened his mouth –

And was hit in the back of his head by a fekkin bat. It was enough to make him drop the fairy. That was all she needed, and she disappeared in a cloud of embers. Furious at losing his prize, he turned, and there was an old witch. And she was holding a violin like a bat. Her eyes were glowing an evil green and she reached back to swing again, but he was faster and gave her a right proper rugby tackle knocking her flat on her back. Then he jumped on her.

"You BITCH! You *bitch*! You hit me!" And he punched her hard. "You made me drop the fairy!" And he punched her again. Her eyes blazed with a furious green fire, but that didn't stop him; he was beyond being stopped. Jared was in his own red rage and he didn't know his own eyes burned purple. She had one hand free and was hitting him, but he was stronger and her punches didn't bother him at all.

The last hit made Caddy's head ring and swung her to the left. She saw the girl's elf knife on the ground where she dropped it. Caddy reached out her free hand and willed the knife to her. It leaped up and flew into her hand with a satisfying smack and in one fluid motion she plunged the knife into the orc's back clear up to the hilt. He jerked up and screamed from the pain of the elf blade and rolled away, but she kept the knife in her hand. She rolled on top, and without thinking she slashed at his neck with one great sweeping motion, and the knife did its work.
His head rolled right off.

And it was done. She was sitting on top of a headless man.

She stood up, shaking from the adrenaline, her chest heaving for air, and gave
the dead body a kick.

"That, you motherfucker, is what you get for interrupting my concert!"

She swayed, and in front of her one of the soldiers ported in. She looked at him and then at the corpse and said, "I need a shower. Can you take me home?"

"Yes, Ms Caddy." And one second later she was there.

_____

Caddy

There were, as there are after every mission that has a glitch, lessons to be learnt.

Lesson one is that they don't need every single elf in existence at a rebirthing; the mob of them was getting too hard to watch and the soldiers couldn't protect such a large group. The little girl, a teenager really, should not have been off by herself. There were so many elves that some were just there to see if one of their relatives made it out and there was no point to that. They could wait in Safe Haven to see who was in the next batch.

Lesson two, and this was the elves talking among themselves, was that it was a disaster that Caddy was unattended. She should have been the first one ported out. But the soldiers were dealing with the two orcs who ran in and then running around rounding up the rest of the elves to get them the hell out of there.

If the little girl had died that would have been a tragedy for one family and one clan, but if Caddy had died –

Well, that would have been a tragedy for all elves. They had lived through the deaths of a great many lords and yet they were still acting like this one very unhealthy lord could take care of herself and if she couldn't, all they'd have to do was set a pie on the windowsill and lure another one in. She was the only one who could call up elves and they had almost lost her.

Caddy's black eye was painful, but she got over it fast. The elves took her
close call very hard.

Ellen, the PR team, and the security group oversaw a cleanup and monitored all of the police communications. The two orc brothers were ported immediately to the Great Yarmouth beach and they walked home with a wild story no one believed. After all, they were high.

The headless corpse was disposed of by the elves. No one ever saw it again. As far as the world was concerned, Jared walked out one night, got high, and never returned. It happens.

Caddy had roused sixty-three elves, so as far as she was concerned it was a good night, and she said so during breakfast the next day. Any night she came out of a bar fight with nothing more than a black eye was a good one. That big lug could've broken her hip, or worse, her hand.

She was actually rather smug about it. There she was, a little old lady, and she fought off an orc and cut off his head. Not too shabby really.

Norma popped in and gave Caddy some medicine for her eye and told her that it would be cleared up by tomorrow, and Caddy got up from the table to take her old bones back to bed. On her way out she turned to Tony and asked how many elves were awake now. She didn't know how many the elves had woken up by themselves.

"As of this morning, Ms Caddy, we have 1,453 elves awake. That is about 20 clans. "

"Goodness! No wonder I keep running into people I don't know! Safe Haven must have a lot of flowering pots now!"

"Yes, Ms Caddy, it's looking much better."

She nodded, happy with that, and went to bed.

Caddy

Caddy was fussing. She had lost a guitar and now a violin, and she was surfing through catalogues to get a replacement for both. She really didn't want to buy one sight unseen and, oh my goodness, the prices! It was crazy money to get a new violin. They cost as much as a car.

Norma brought in Tony to reassure the lord that, yes, just get what you want. For that money the retailers will bring a couple to the house for her to personally try out. Or the elves could just make one for her.

Caddy knew they were correct, but she just wasn't used to spending money on herself like that. On other people, yes, she had no problems. But on herself? That wasn't how she was brought up and certainly wasn't how she had lived when Ricky was alive. That destroyed violin was almost 50 years old, and she saved her pennies for two years to buy it. Then the fridge broke down; oh boy did they ever have a row over using "their" money for the fridge and leaving "her" violin money stashed in a shoebox! From Ricky's point of view they needed a new fridge and using savings was silly when there was cash in a shoebox earmarked for a toy.

But she bought the violin, and he was forced to cash in a bond for the fridge. And even though they had plenty of money in savings, to both of them it was the principle of the thing. Money was always about control and that violin was a sore point between them for years. Now she had bashed the hard head of an orc with the treasured instrument and she felt guilty about replacing it.

It was late, so she sent all of the elves home, and she sat in the sitting room brooding over the violin. The wind howled and it was a horrible night out which matched her mood, so she sat down at the piano and played on that for a while.

She enjoyed the piano, and living alone now she didn't have to hold back because of other people's sensitive ears. Caddy played some jazz to loosen up and then went into a bit of rock which was fun and lightened her mood. Then into swing. Swing was just a happy genre, and she played as loud as she wanted and belted out "Begin the Beguine" just like it was 1944. That was so much fun she played it twice.

The wind was howling outside, and she was howling inside and really pushing those notes —

There was a knock on the door. Not really a knock; someone was pounding on it.

Sighing and not a little irritated she went to answer it. Who could it possibly be at this time of night and in this horrible weather? It wouldn't be an elf. They'd just port in without knocking.

She turned on the porch light, swung open the door, and there stood a monster.

It was huge – at least two metres tall – and covered in seaweed. It raised its arms, and she then discovered there was a naked man under all that sea foliage because the leaves couldn't hide all of his important parts. Suddenly he ROARED something in Elvish, and then he very, very slowly fell on her.

Caddy screamed and tried to back away, but he was massive and she was caught in the seaweed and tangled in his waving arms. He sagged forward and she could see he was really passing out and she was just in the way. She screamed again and tried to hold him up, but he was just too heavy and she slowly sank under his wet, seaweedy weight. He stank like a dead fish.

This time she yelled for Tony or Vernon or *someone* to come and help her! Immediately two soldiers and Tony popped in, and it was all the small men could do to lever the monster-man off her enough for her to crawl out from underneath him.

Two more soldiers popped in, and then Vernon, who must have been in the bath because he was naked and only had a towel wrapped around him. Which was better than seaweed,
giving more coverage.

"*Who* is this!? *What* is this!?" cried Caddy. Her little entry hall was stuffed from side to side with the man. She could see it was a man now, and every extra inch of the narrow hall was filled with elves, chattering and exclaiming and ordering each other to do things. A soldier turned the man's head to allow him to breathe and Vernon went pale.

"Neptune! It's Lord Neptune!" He bent down to take a closer look. "I met him once in Before Times. He's not doing well is he?"

"Neptune? This is a lord?" She looked again at the man passed out in her narrow hall, the seaweed, a tiny crab crawling out of his hair and turned to Vernon. "Do you mean like, Neptune, Lord of the Sea Neptune? *That* Neptune?"

"I think there is only one, Ms Caddy." Vernon looked again. "Normally he has a fish tail, but when he's on land he can grow legs."

"Neptune!" Caddy looked again, he looked pretty bad. Gaunt. His skin was a sickly blue and his beard was a mess.

"What the hell am I supposed to do with a Neptune!"

The elves looked at her. They didn't know what to do with him either.

Caddy scratched her head and made a decision.

"Take him up to my bedroom, and put him to bed. Thank goodness it's king size. We need a doctor type elf to look at him and see if he's ill or whatever and get him sorted. Can you guys get him up there?"

Vernon shrugged. "Sure, we've handled plenty of drunk lords; we can haul them around."

"Do you think he's drunk?"

"No, my guess is that the pain and exhaustion from morphing (and he doesn't look to be very healthy now) just got to be too much for him. We can fix him up Ms Caddy, don't you worry."

"Okay, then. Let's get this party started. You'll be working on him all night, I can see that now. I'll go sleep in the spare bedroom."

She turned and went upstairs and didn't wait to see what the elves did. They would deal with Neptune whether she was there or not.

"Neptune! I can't believe –" Caddy stopped halfway up the stairs and turned. "I want a guard on his door. I don't want him wandering around the house unescorted."

"Yes, Ms Caddy!"

And then she went to bed, still mumbling to herself.

Neptune

During the night, there was a lot of noise she could hear in her bedroom and Caddy kept waking up to banging and yelling and quite a bit of elvish cursing. Her spare bedroom was directly over her usual bedroom and there was no soundproofing in these old houses.

After a fitful night, she was up with the sparrows and down in the kitchen eating her breakfast when Norma and another elf popped in.

"Ms Caddy, this is Nathan." Nathan nodded shyly and bowed.

"Nathan is a healer and he's been to see Lord Neptune."

Caddy smiled and nodded.

"Have a seat, Nathan. It's so nice to meet you! What do you think about my houseguest?"

The elf sat down. He was a bald man with a pleasant bland expression and a body as round as a body could get. Caddy bet if he fell down he would just roll.

"He's just ill from neglect, Ms Caddy. He wanted to find you, and of course he had to walk on land, so when he made his legs he simply used up everything he had. I think he thought he was stronger than he really was and just overextended. So we need to get him to eat so his body has something to work with, he needs to practise his abilities, and he should be just fine in two or three days."

"Well, that sounds encouraging. What do you mean by 'practise his abilities'? What is that?"

Nathan considered this. "I really don't know what his abilities are, but I bet it means moving water around. We're land elves and historically haven't had anything to do with the sea. If this were the Before Times we'd hand him over to merfolk and they would know what to do. So we're flying a bit blind now."

Caddy nodded. "I suppose he'll tell us. But in the meantime I'm sure we can get some food in him. Has anyone taken a tray up yet?"

"That's the problem, Ms Caddy," Norma said. "We took some soup up, and he wouldn't eat it. He was quite rude. It's what we would normally feed a lord who needs building up. We feed it to you all the time, and you like it, but he doesn't."

"You've been feeding me *medicine*?"

"Not medicine, per se. Healthy food with a few extra herbs in it. Chicken noodle soup. You like it and it's doing you a world of good. Between that and your practising, you are much healthier than you were when you first met Tony. He says you were on your last legs!"

Caddy looked at Norma and then back at her breakfast porridge, and sure enough, she never noticed it before but there were some tiny bits of green in there. Then she shrugged. She did feel much better. She didn't look in mirrors, but even sitting here and looking at her hands she could see that the fingers were almost totally straight now and the age spots had faded to a few freckles.

"Maybe he doesn't like chicken noodle soup. He's half a fish. I don't think soup is an under-the-sea sort of dish. For one thing, it would be very watery. " Caddy ate a bit of porridge and thought about what to feed a sea lord. "Let's try some sashimi. Let's feed him some mermaid comfort food. Fish roe? That might get him started."

Norma leaned forward. "Would you take up the tray, Ms Caddy? I think he would be much more polite to you. Maybe make more of an effort to eat to please you."

Caddy nodded and the elves popped away before she could change her mind or offer an alternative. She finished up her oatmeal, and the more she ate the more green bits she found floating in it. Caddy wondered what it was.

Neptune

Neptune sat up in the bed and watched the traffic go down the road. It was fascinating what these humans did. He had seen some of their magical carts going across bridges and on piers, but he was much closer now, and like the ships that didn't use sails to catch the wind, these things used some sort of shit burning process to make them move. Five hundred years ago humans and orcs were still using the same methods to move things around that they had for millennia and he comes back now and look at this! It was quite a change.

On the side table was a bowl of cold soup. It was hot when the little elf brought it in, but it was inedible and he told her so. The old Neptune would have thrown it back at her but the new Neptune understood she was just trying her best. So he merely pushed it away
and told her to fuck off.

There was a soft knock at the door. Neptune looked at who was making the noise, and nothing happened. A minute passed and there was another rap on the door. What were they doing out there? A minute passed, and then he heard three very deliberate raps, quite loud.

"What are you –," he yelled, and the door flew
open, " – doing out there.
Stop that infernal noise!"

In the doorway stood the female lord. He knew it
was her because her green eyes glowed with irritation. She
was carrying an enormous tray; it was heavy and she had to
turn
sideways to walk in.

"Good morning, Lord Neptune. I hope you slept
well." And she walked over to the table with the cold soup
on it and gave him a look. She wanted him to do
something. What was he supposed to do? She waited and
then gave an audible sigh.

"Could you please move the bowl, Lord Neptune?
This blasted tray is heavy. " She looked at him and
frowned. "To the floor gently, please, would be good. *Do
not throw it.*
I don't want the mess."

Never in his life had Neptune been spoken to that
way. No one had ever asked him to move anything much
less acted as if he was a child who didn't know how to
wipe his own arse.

He moved the bowl with well-practised ability and set it down where she said, gently.

She set the tray on the table with an "oof" and stood back and rubbed her arms. "They always overload these things." She turned and smiled, and it was as if the sun came out. She was not healthy, he could see that, but when she smiled you forgot how old and worn she was and you could see what she once looked like. And what she could look like when she healed properly.

He hadn't said a word yet, not even a morning greeting, and he suddenly had no idea how to start. How many women had he had in his long long life? Thousands? More? He always knew what to say and do, but this one made him tongue-tied and unsure, and he had no idea why.

Well, that was going to stop now. He was Neptune, an Elemental Lord and deserving of respect, and she was not going to intimidate him with a smile.

He cleared his throat, opened his mouth to give her a morning greeting, and all that came out was a squeak. It was embarrassing and he turned bright red.

"Sorry." By all the gods, he was apologising to her!

She smiled, this time with sympathy. "You made a huge roar when you came in last night. And you yelled at the door. It probably strained your voice. You need to build up your strength." And with that she bent to the tray, found a little plate, and piled it high with different kinds of raw fish. The tray was heavy with all types of sushi and sashimi arranged very prettily in a starburst. Neptune was suddenly very, very hungry and his sea-blue eyes gleamed.

"I like tuna, but what do you like? White fish? Eel?"

"Tuna."

She picked up a bit of tuna with two sticks and before he knew what was happening she poked it in his mouth. Then she picked up another piece and ate it. And that's what they did for the next hour. She would pick up a piece of something, explain what it was, ask if he liked it (and he never said no), and they would share. She showed him how to dip in soy sauce, which he liked very much, and even had him try a bit of wasabi that made her eyes water. She gasped, which made him laugh.

When the tray was empty and he had a full belly, she stood up and said, "I have work to do, and you need to rest now. I'll be back in a couple of hours for dinner. If you have to shit or pee, *do not* do it in bed. An elf is going to sit in here just in case you need anything at all, and they will take you to the toilet." Smiled that gorgeous smile again and nodded to him. "I'll be back soon." Then she was gone.

Neptune lay back and stared at the ceiling. He could talk perfectly well, but he couldn't force out two words to this woman. He never did ask her name. Or say thank you.

He would the next time she came around and with that thought he slept.

―――――――――――――――――――――

Caddy

Norma asked how it went, and Caddy shrugged.

"He seemed a bit stunned really. Didn't say much. Just kept staring at me like my hair was on fire and I didn't have the sense to notice it."

The elf laughed. "He's a lord, Ms Caddy. In ten thousand years, I doubt if anyone has ever said more to him than "Yes, Lord". He just holds out his hand and someone puts a beer in it. They're very spoiled. Did you ask him to do anything?"

"I asked him to move a bowl so I could put the damn tray down."

Norma went into gales of laughter. "He probably didn't know what to do! What *should* I do? What is this moving thing you ask? Put it *where*?"

Caddy grinned. "Well, he wasn't that easy to confuse. He did move it. Just a flick of a finger and the bowl went exactly where it needed to go and without spilling a drop of soup. He didn't even have to think about it. I wish I could do that!"

"Oh, you will, Ms Caddy, you will. Neptune is very ancient. He's had a lot of practice." Norma laughed. "If he's going to get better he needs to work and exercise his abilities. But I heard he's very lazy, so he might be here for a while!"

Caddy looked at Norma and raised an eyebrow. "Oh, I'll make him practise. I'm not going to wait on him hand and foot for more than a couple of days. Two or three days is what the healer said and I'm keeping to that schedule."

_____

Neptune

There was a knock on the door, and this time Neptune knew what was going to happen. The woman would be in with a tray of food and they would feed again.

Being prepared this time, he said, "Enter!" And she did. She had a tray, and this time there were two bowls on it and a pitcher.

"Good afternoon! Did you have a nice nap?"

He smiled back. "Yes." Then he paused. "Thank you."

She put the tray down, and there was an amused glint in her bright green eyes. It suddenly occurred to him that he couldn't remember the last time he saw a female lord close up. He stayed in the sea with his merfolk and they were all he needed. He had stopped going to Gaia's boring ceremonies millennia ago and he didn't party with other lords. They didn't want to get wet and he didn't want to bother with legs. Maybe that's why he was so intimidated; he wasn't used to being with a peer.

Caddy looked at the big man. He seemed a bit better already. He was still gaunt but not quite as blue.

"Thank me later. You might change your mind." She gestured at the tray. "We're going to do a little physio-therapy. The elves say you need to practise and get the energy flowing to get better, so that's what we're going to do. Or rather, that's what *you* are going to do."

"Get my energy flowing?" She was bold for a woman, but if that's what she wanted –

And he patted the bed and smiled his most winning smile.

The woman lord laughed at him. She laughed a lot. It was rather insulting, really.

"Sorry, Neptune, you're not getting lucky." And when she settled down to an occasional giggle, she told him what she wanted him to do. She poured water from the jug into one bowl and set the other empty bowl on the furthest window sill. He was to take as much water as he wanted – or as little – and move it from one bowl to the other. Only the water. He wasn't to spill a drop. Not a single one. When he was done they would have dinner.

Neptune was sulky. This was not how he liked to get his energy flowing. This was work. And ridiculously easy. Not that he had ever done such a thing before because it was a useless skill, but it was going to be easy.

"This is stupid."

"Then do it and get it over with. Dinner waits!"

And then she pulled her trump card.

"I'll wager you can't."

Neptune's eyes got wide and he grinned. A bet! That was one she would lose!

"For what prize?" he asked.

"What do you want? What would make it interesting for you?"

He thought. If he asked for a kiss she would say no and laugh at him again. Then he hit on it.

"A song. You sing me a song."

She smiled and nodded. "And what do I get if you lose?"

"My abject humiliation and a bowl of water?"

And she laughed and laughed. "Yes, that will be a good prize!"

He grinned, delighted he had made her laugh with a proper joke. "Watch!"

Neptune frowned and felt the water with his mind. Easy to do. Then he –

– suddenly realised this was going to be much harder than he thought. The water was slippery and when he thought he had it in one compact blob bits would drop off and the task was that not a drop would be spilled out of the bowls.

He made the blob smaller. He would do it in two turns. That was still within the rules.

Caddy watched the water swirl and form a ball and float over the bowl, but it would drip. He couldn't let it drip on the floor as he flew it over to the other bowl. That would mean he lost.

He frowned and his blue eyes glowed bright. This was the first time she had ever seen a lord work and it was enthralling. Beads of sweat formed on his face. He was not going to let the task defeat him and he was not going to lose the bet. He used a smaller amount of water in an attempt to control the entire surface of the blob and prevent it from dripping. Still too big.

He quartered it. Then halved that again and he had a size he could manage.

The ball of water flew to the other side of the room and gently fell into the other bowl; not a drop was lost in between bowls. Neptune repeated the process until all the water was transferred. He fell back onto the bed and his chest was heaving.

"Good for you! You won!"

He grinned, but he didn't sit up. He was exhausted.

"No, *you* won didn't you?"

"Yes, but we won't quibble. I'll go get your dinner and I'll sing you a song afterwards."

Dinner was bream with sea vegetables which they both loved and boiled potatoes which Neptune didn't eat. Caddy showed him how to use a fork and knife, which he thought was a bit fussy, but he was willing to try.

Caddy asked him a lot of questions about his life as Neptune, the merfolk, and how he moved the water from bowl to bowl.

The merfolk questions were easy to answer, but it was hard for him to explain how he moved the water because he just did it. But he tried his best to articulate what he was doing. No one had ever asked him before *how* he did anything, and he had never thought about the technical aspects. She listened intently and it was very flattering to have this fellow lord so interested in his abilities. The merfolk never asked him if what he did was hard or how he did it or if it hurt afterwards. They didn't ask him much, really, other than what fish he wanted for dinner.

After dinner, she sang two songs, but while it was very nice, it wasn't anything any highly skilled human or mermaid couldn't do. So he asked her about her abilities.

"I've talked to you about what I can do. You didn't use any ability to sing tonight, although you have a wonderful voice. What made your songs travel so far? How did you do it?"

Caddy tilted her head and narrowed her eyes. "My abilities are not the music. The song is just a carrier. It's a way for me to focus and concentrate on sound waves. Everything is made of energy and energy comes in waves. I am learning to control waves in sound and in light.

Because I'm a musician, I like to work with sound, but I can do a few things with reflections and light. When I want to I can sing in a way that creates vibrations and waves, and those waves can go very very far if you push them hard enough. My abilities are very new to me and all I can do are
some simple things."

"Like what? I thought the water trick was going to be simple because I can make a tidal wave if I want, but it wasn't because it was subtle. What's simple to you?"

She looked around, saw the bowl of water, and carried it to the table next to the bed.

"Now this is too heavy for me to move like you did yesterday. That's a different skill and I'm still learning that one. But here is a skill I've just learned. Watch the water."

Neptune bent over to watch. She frowned and concentrated on the water in the bowl, and her eyes glowed green. It began to vibrate. He could see tiny ripples on the water's surface as it vibrated from inside the bowl. Suddenly it boiled up and evaporated, all in the space of a few seconds. The bowl was empty with just a leftover wisp of steam rising up from the centre.

Neptune's eyes widened. "You heated it?"

"I boiled it with sound. You couldn't hear it, but all sound waves are a form of energy and energy generates heat. "

He sat back and thought about what that meant. And then he looked at her closely.

"But you haven't used that ability much have you? You said it's new to you."

"Neptune, I've only been really using my abilities consciously for about five months now. I think I've been using them subconsciously for years and maybe that little tiny bit of ability practice is what kept me alive so long."

"Every time I wake up elves, every time I work hard, every time I push myself, I get a little bit stronger and learn a little bit more. I think it's the musician's training in me to constantly practise, to get a tiny bit better, to push to learn a new chord or reach a new note. But, Neptune," and her voice lowered to a whisper, "it scares me, too. I worry about losing control."

He nodded; he understood that. "You practise to make yourself stronger but also to control the power you release. Gaia had great power, but I wonder sometimes if she really meant to kill everyone who was with her that day. I wonder if she just lost control."

"Yes, that's what I'm afraid of, and that's what holds me back. I don't want to start something and end up with a chain reaction I can't control, so I'm very careful. I'll keep practising because that's what I do; maybe one day I'll pick up a bowl of soup and move it like you did."

She smiled and got up. "Anyway, enough for tonight. This has been a very interesting conversation. Good night, Neptune." And she turned and went to the door.

"Good night!"

She stopped at the door and smiled. "My name is Caddy, Neptune." And she shut the door behind her.

Caddy

Caddy didn't sleep well. Orcs were chasing her elves. Tony, Norma, all of them, and when they were caught the orcs would pick them up by the scruff of their necks, and then the orcs would open their huge, gaping mouths –

And she woke up in a cold sweat. It took her a long time to get back to sleep.

Wendell

For three days Wendell sat on the bench on the corner of Waterloo Road and London Road South where he had a good view of The Rum Lot's door and pretended to play a game on his phone. Winning at Minecraft wasn't his goal; taking a photo of an elf was. So far he had had no luck at all, but he was determined to get one.

When he showed his Magic Card to Ms Caddy and the elf popped in he was gobsmacked. Then she got up to leave, turned and winked at him and then disappeared, he almost shit his shorts. But when that girl elf came to work the till and asked if she could help him all Wendell could do was turn and run.

He ran all the way home, burst through the front door, ran into his grubby bedroom, threw himself on his bed and hyperventilated for a good ten minutes. All of his life, for as long as he could remember, he was obsessed with elves, fairies, and all the magical creatures that inhabited myth and legend. He read every book and story from *The Smith and the Devil* to Tolkien, played thousands of fantasy games of all types, cosplayed and watched every movie. He was the acknowledged expert in his group on folklore.

And now he saw not one but three magical beings in one day.

Of course, when he was back under control he texted everyone in his gaming group and told them what had just happened, and to his shock not a single one of his so-called friends believed him. Even Jilly who claimed she had seen fairies.

Wotcha smokin?
No way
bro , u r kray z
Short ppl r not *elf emoji*

No one believed him. Not a single person believed him that there were elves operating a shop on London Road in ordinary, absolutely average, unmagical Lowestoft.

Even his mother didn't believe him. When he told her he thought she was going to cry.

His family loved their kind, handsome, aimless son but despaired that the only thing he was interested in was useless. Working as a zero-hour stocker at Asda wasn't getting him anywhere either. He was twenty-one, lived at home in his childhood bedroom, worked at Asda three nights a week, and was obsessed with fantasy during the day. If he could show his mum and dad a photo maybe he could prove he wasn't useless.

After three days he noticed a couple of things. First was that the many customers who entered the shop were always smiling when they came out, but not one seemed excited or shocked at what they found there.

When they walked by no one mentioned elves. Second, he saw that a couple people couldn't go in. They would walk *to* the shop and simply seem to glide by and miss the door. Then they would look back, turn around, and head towards it, and walk right past again. Wendell saw a man in a suit do that at least three times before he gave up.

On the third day, he saw an elf. A man walking his dog had allowed the dog to poop right in front of the shop and didn't clean it up; after he left an elf came out and took care of the poo. Wendell took about a dozen pics and even had time to get a few seconds of video.

Nothing showed up in the pictures. Each photo had a picture of the front of the shop with a blurry blob that moved around but could be anything. The video was the same. You could see the blob move and the poo get bagged but no details that told you what the blob was. Cars, people walking by, everything else was crystal clear.

To Wendell that was proof of magic, but he knew it wouldn't be proof to anyone else.

He looked up from his phone and almost dropped it. There was an elf sitting on the other end of his bench also watching the shop.

The little man was built like a weightlifter. He was wearing a plain dark green uniform, a dark green peaked cap with a very flashy red feather on it, and he had a sword. His beard was long and braided and tucked into his shirt. He was drinking coffee from a Starbucks cup and paid no attention to Wendell at all.

Wendell froze. He didn't know what to do and was deathly afraid that if he moved the elf would disappear.

The elf took another sip of coffee and ignored the boy.

"Nice sword."

The elf slowly turned to look at Wendell and then turned back to observe the shop. His eyes were as cold and deadly as a viper. He took another sip of his coffee. For the first time in his life Wendell knew he was sitting next to a man who could and would kill him without a second thought.

Then he was gone. The coffee cup, however, stayed.

Victor

"It's not possible, Lord Cadence. He can't."

Caddy looked at the soldier. His name was Victor, and behind him stood his senior and another soldier. She said nothing. She didn't smile or try to put him at ease but simply
raised an eyebrow.

"You have been specially recommended for this task, Victor."

Victor turned to his senior and growled, "Thanks for nothing." The senior looked away.

"Lord Cadence, please. He's a human –"

Caddy nodded. "That's obvious. And I know why you aren't happy with the human race, but, Victor, I have plans for this one, and you're the man who I was told was the best to teach him. I can look for someone else if you won't take the job."

She leaned forward. "So, Victor, I'm asking you. *Can't* take the job or *won't* take the job?"

Victor's jaw twitched. He would never, in front of his brother soldiers, say that he couldn't. And he would never say to a lord he wouldn't.

So he popped out. No answer, no bow, he just left.

Caddy turned to the two remaining soldiers and said, "He'll do it. Watch them both for me, will you? Call me if I need to make an appearance. Make sure he doesn't torture the boy too much. A broken man will do us no good."

She returned to her sudoku and the two soldiers bowed and popped out.

_____

Wendell

The elf popped back to the bench and picked up his coffee and took a sip.

Wendell sat very quiet and didn't say a word.

"Lord Cadence," the elf said, without looking at Wendell, "has ordered me to teach you. Be at Fen Park at five o'clock tomorrow morning. Wear workout clothes."

"Teach me what?" Wendell suddenly had wild visions of magic and wizards.

The elf looked at him, and if his flat black eyes held any emotion, it wasn't love.

"To be a Ranger, whatever the shit that is."

And he popped out.

Neptune

Neptune burst into the kitchen like a man-sized hurricane. Caddy sat working on an online crossword puzzle and eating her breakfast of porridge with the green bits floating in it.

The only thing the lord was wearing was an incensed expression on his face.

"I WILL NOT WEAR BREECHES!"

Behind him popped Tony, Vernon, and two other elves who were almost buried under the load of clothes they were carrying.

Caddy looked up. "Obviously you aren't wearing breeches. Why not?"

"Neptune does not wear breeches. How the fuck am I supposed to shit in these things?" And he threw a pair at Tony.

That was a mistake because before he could take another breath, Caddy flew across the room, eyes blazing in absolute fury. She barely came up to his shoulder, but she poked him in the chest so hard with her finger he had to step back.

"YOU WILL NOT ABUSE MY ELVES! You will not yell at them (poke), throw things at them (poke), or do anything other than treat them with respect! DO YOU UNDERSTAND!"

Neptune opened his mouth, but Caddy wasn't done yet.

"These elves have been asleep for 3,500 years. Where have you been? Asleep for 3,500 years. Now you're waking up to a world with dangers NONE of you can comprehend. Lords – great, fucking magical lords – were wiped out by savages with bows and arrows. Elves were decimated and driven to hibernation. Now they, and you, are waking up in a world you don't know anything about. I do. "

She took a breath. Neptune tried again. "Caddy, I – "

Too late; she still wasn't done. The elves in the kitchen were frozen, their eyes as wide as saucers.

"Neptune, there are only two lords on Earth now. Neither of us are in the best of shape. There are a little over a thousand elves – "

"Three thousand two hundred fifty-six," interrupted Tony and for his pains he got a withering look from Caddy.

" –but there were three BILLION people on this planet when you woke up! THREE BILLION! How many of them are orcs, Neptune?

They have weapons that harness the sun. They can kill every one of us in a few days if they put their minds to it. I woke these elves and, by all the gods out there, I'm going to make sure they have their place in this world and bring back Balance, and no one, not even the great and mighty Neptune, is going to get in my way. If you think I'm going to allow you to mess up this work because you have wardrobe issues, think again.

"Neptune, the only way balance can be brought back is to work with humans – the good ones – and in the meantime we need to integrate inside of their culture and do our best not to scare them. When they get scared they get nasty, as you well know (poke). That means following their customs when we are in their world, and one of their customs is that a man keeps his sword sheathed when in public and his weapon doesn't come out until it's being used. When I teach you how to use a fork I'm not being prissy; I'm teaching you survival skills. When an elf *who is looking out for you* gives you a pair of trousers you do not complain that your balls can't breathe. He's trying to keep you alive."

She stopped and glared right into his eyes and he glared into hers – and he broke. He held out his hand for the trousers and an elf gave them back to him.

Caddy swung around and plopped in her chair.

"Besides, you have a very nice dick, and you know that if you meet human ladies they won't be able to keep their eyes off it. Give them a chance to keep their emotions in check and let's not make their husbands jealous."

Neptune stalked out of the kitchen without a word. Caddy heard him go up the stairs to the bedroom and slam the door.

"Tony. Try finding some elastic banded swimming trunks, loose ones, for Neptune. Or a kilt."

"Yes, Ms Caddy."

Caddy

Caddy decided to walk to the shop today. Sure, she could have had an elf port her, but she wanted to walk down the Prom and clear her head. It was one of Lowestoft's rare clear days when the grey sea sparkled in the morning light.

Some of what she said to Neptune Caddy had never articulated before. She had, in many ways, been operating on instinct. But when Caddy said, "I'm going to make sure they have their place in this world," she absolutely meant it. She would not fail them.

When she was a teacher, every summer she would work during her "time off". She would look at where she wanted her class to be next June. What concerts would they play in, what contests, what songs were the best to choose and spend their time on to win? Which students would return to her music classes? What were their talents, and what were their weaknesses, and how would they align with the goals of the group?

Then, looking at her goals for the last day of the school year and working backwards, she would make a methodical plan to get there. Ricky always said, the goal makes the strategy, but how you got to the goal was tactics. She needed to think how she was going to get the elves happily and safely integrated in this world, and the only way she was going to be successful would be to plan, practise, and execute. She needed to plan out some workable tactics.

Of course, teaching kids to play *Jingle Bells* on the violin for the Christmas concert was one thing, but integrating elves in a new world filled with very dangerous humans and orcs was quite another. No one ever died in one of her Parent's Night concerts. Not that she knew of.

"Hello, Lord Caddy."

Turning, she saw Jack the raven, sitting on the back of a bench. She took a seat on the bench, and he hopped over to the low wall that stopped tourists, lords, and ravens from tumbling down the cliff to the beach below.

"Hiya, Jack! A lovely morning isn't it?"

Jack nodded, but he was not there to talk about the weather.

"Ms Caddy, did I see Neptune in your bedroom window? Was it really him?"

Caddy didn't even bother to ask how a raven knew who Neptune was. Now if Jack were a seagull that would make more sense. But she just nodded.

Jack tilted his head to see her better, fluffed his feathers, and then preened. He was thinking.

"Where has Neptune been all these years? I've never seen a merfolk around here."

"He said he was asleep in a very deep, very cold place and only came up every five hundred years or so to check on the world. He says the merfolk have disappeared, and it was my singing that woke him up, so he followed the songs to me."

"Ah, that makes sense."

"Really. My story makes sense? You must be kidding, Jack One-Eye."

He cackled. "It makes as much sense as talking to ravens Lord Cadence Aeldor!"

"What should I know about him, Jack?"

"Neptune is a man of huge appetites and for all his love for his merfolk, a loner, so I'm not surprised he is alone now and has been alone all along. But I'm surprised he's on land; he hates the land."

"And he loves his merfolk, isn't that right, Jack?"

"He loves his merfolk over anything or anyone, Ms Caddy."

"I thought that, Jack. I could hear that in his voice when he talked to me about them."

"Are you going to wake them up? He'll ask you to."

"Of course he will; that's why he's here. I never thought he followed my song across the seven seas to ask me to share my Spotify playlist. But he's also lonely, I think."

"I see he is in your bedroom."

"If you're asking if I'm fucking him, the answer is no you nosy bird. I'm a bit old for that nonsense, and besides, he'd probably crush me or break a hip or something. The man is huge."

"Oh, you're not too old, Ms Caddy. No one is. And besides, you are healthier every time I see you." Jack paused. "The elves will be worried about him, that you'll run off with him
and forget them."

"The elves or you, Jack?"

"Both."

Caddy looked at the sea. It was lovely. "I'll do my best about the merfolk. But whatever happens, Jack, I know what my job is. I know what I need to do. I didn't wake up 3,000 elves to abandon them to be eaten by orcs. Neither you nor the elves need worry."

Jack nodded. "Thank you, Ms Caddy, for reassuring me. He's a charming man, and the ladies all loved him. "

"Yes, I can see the attraction. I admit he's fascinating. I've never met a lord before!" Caddy looked at Jack and smiled, "Would you like me to buy you a bucket of KFC, you cannibal?"

Jack was wise enough to know she was done talking about Neptune.

"When they open, Ms Caddy, that would be very kind. Legs, please."

Caddy

Behind the till counter were two doors. One led to a closet-sized coffee area and a loo; the other door led to a small stock room. Where there was once a shelf now stood a plain but very heavy security door with a palm print reader in the centre and single bare lightbulb over it.

Elves, by some magic that bent space, had built a massive office area on the other side. Most elves ported in and didn't bother with the door, but it was there just in case Caddy or Ellen wanted to get in without disturbing an elf.

Caddy, along with an ever-growing staff of elves, had an office back there. It was a lovely cosy office with a fake window (probably some sort of mundane TV screen) that looked out over the road and changed with the season and weather outside, a huge and ancient wood desk, comfy chairs, a computer, and even a working fireplace.

She spent the morning typing in random thoughts and questions and a rough draft of her plan to bring elves into the modern world as a unified force and borderless nation that didn't claim any land. In Before Times, elves lived in isolated, fragmented clans and were forced to stay in one area because of *terrior* and so each clan could be overwhelmed by a sheer mass of humans and orcs. Caddy needed to get them to work as one if they were going to survive, and she needed to make sure they had allies inside the human community.

Once she had a plan roughed in she would talk over the various aspects with
committees of elves.

There's nothing like a good plan to give one the illusion of control, Caddy thought.

Well-pleased to be doing something positive, she broke for lunch and had an elf port her back home, where Neptune was waiting at the kitchen table.

He was wearing a utility kilt. And a neatly pressed shirt. And knee socks and shoes.

"Ohhh! You look very smart!" Caddy gushed, but it was true. "Stand up and let me have a look at you!" Neptune grinned and stood up so she could get the full effect.

"I'm told the northern humans wear these. Scottish kilts. I don't have to wear underwear if I don't want to!"

"Always a plus." Caddy felt the material and looked at him from all sides, cooing and complimenting until he was quite puffed up.

"Let's have lunch, and if you want, we'll take a walk on the Prom just to get out a bit."

Neptune agreed, and that's what they did. An hour later they were walking on the Promenade, and while Neptune was charming and attentive, he also kept looking at the sea. Caddy knew he missed it terribly. He wouldn't go down on the beach, and when she asked why he said it was too risky. Once he got on sand that was damp from real seawater he might involuntarily turn back into his merman body. Then turning back to a human body would be very painful. It was best he stayed away. For now.

They held hands as they walked along. It was a lovely day, and while it was still chilly, there were plenty of people strolling with dogs, old people on mobility scooters, and young families with children.

She bought them both huge soft ice cream cones at the Claremont, and they found a bench overlooking the beach where they sat and enjoyed them. Caddy noticed with amusement some of the sideways glances Neptune got from the young and not-so-young ladies. He was film-star handsome – and, oh, that kilt!

"I've been thinking," she started.

"Will this involve poking me in the chest?"

"No. Probably not."

He nodded and levitated a glob of melted ice-cream before it landed on his kilt.

"Anyway, I thought about singing to your merfolk and seeing if they'll come to me like elves do. I thought I might try tomorrow night. What do you think about –"

He didn't say a word but bent down to kiss her full on the lips leaving Caddy quite breathless when it was all done.

"I guess that's a yes?"

"Thank you, Caddy."

"Don't thank me yet, I've not done anything, and I might not succeed. I will try."

He finished his cone, and he hugged her again, pulling her close, and she leaned into him. They sat on the bench for a long time like that.

_____

Caddy

That night, Neptune sat in on a meeting with Caddy, Vernon, Norma, and Thomas, the head of the soldier elves. In the last few days he had heard their stories about the Before Times and what the elves went through, but that seemed long ago. Now, listening to them plan, he understood that while no one was massing to attack elves now, the risks never went away. They were in a ceasefire; the war was not over.

Neptune listened and learned as they debated the pros and cons of various beaches, how to set the guard so that Caddy would be safe, and the issues that had arisen the last time she sang resulting in the fight with an orc. If his merfolk came back, as he dearly hoped they would, he would face the same threats.

Neptune thought they would just walk down to the South Beach to the wide sands nearest to Caddy's house, but the elf soldiers were spooked now. Between patrolling policemen, possible orcs, and the random unknown human dog walker they didn't want anyone around the lord, for miles if they could manage it.

"Ms Caddy, if you die we all die. We just can't let anything happen again like that. Great Yarmouth was just too close a call." Thomas continued, "Our problem now is that while my lads are great warriors, there aren't many of us who've made it through to hibernation."

When Neptune heard how close Caddy was to getting killed that night his stomach flipped, and he wholeheartedly agreed with Thomas' words. They couldn't let that happen again.

Thomas looked at Neptune. "Most of us soldiers died defending the villages. There's only about fifteen of us left in our clan area, so we're spread pretty thin.

"We're limited by *terrior*, like any other elf, so we can't travel too far looking for the perfect beach. Does it have to be on a beach? The humans have their beachside caravan parks everywhere now. Can't we do this somewhere inland, like the Carlton Marshes or around Benacre?"

Shaking her head, Caddy explained that it had to be on water. That's where she sang before, and it worked because she could send out vibrations directly in the water.

After looking at Google maps and debating the pros and cons they settled on a stretch of beach south of Pakefield that still had farmers' fields behind the cliffs and no houses nearby. Thomas and Vernon would check it out in person in the morning, and the awakening group would go there the next morning just after midnight. Neptune would watch everything from the cliff just in case something dire happened and he needed to intervene, but otherwise he would stay away from the sea.

The elves all went home, and Caddy and Neptune sat on the sofa together and watched a bit of TV. He really liked marine documentaries. During a commercial he suddenly turned to her and said, "Caddy, come upstairs with me." Just like that. No seduction, no wheedling, no build up, no nothing.

Caddy was startled. But of course, they'd been on their way to bed all day. And besides, he smelled really really good.

"Okay."

And they walked upstairs hand in hand.

Caddy, 1945

When Caddy married the first time she had not had sex with a man other than her husband. In 1945, good girls didn't have sex before their wedding day and she was determined not to get pregnant. If she had gotten pregnant she would have had to leave the WRENs, and the humiliation of going back home would just have been too great. She would have failed.

The last thing her father said as she walked out the door the day she left for training was not to come back with any brats because only slags and dykes joined the military. He needn't have worried because she never went back.

She was twenty-one when she married Reggie Jones who owned three fishing boats and somehow managed to keep them going throughout the war.

He was a charmer. He was twice her age, skinny as a rail, and loads of fun. Caddy met him while she was working on a Royal Navy patrol boat out of Grimsby. She was taking a break and leaning on the railing topside, and his fishing boat passed by just metres away. He waved, she waved back, and that was enough of an introduction for him. For some strange reason he thought she was cute despite the fact that the first time he saw her she was in a boiler suit and was filthy from working on a balky engine as a mechanic's helper. He was only the third man in her life to ever buy her a beer at a pub and only the second one she kissed. In the wild night of celebration on VE Day she went to bed with a man for the first time and Reggie must have enjoyed the experience because two weeks later they were married.

Being married meant immediate discharge from the WRENs and Reggie set her up in a nice flat in Lowestoft. He said that it would be better for her to be back in her hometown because he was out to sea fishing so often and he was in port in Lowestoft as often as he was in Grimsby. She didn't understand the logic, but she was besotted with him, and, besides, men knew best. She was married and married women did what their husbands told them to do.

When Reggie was in town they spent most of their time in bed which suited Reggie to a tee. Caddy found that she had a pretty strong libido and she loved the smell and feel of him. She learned quite a few interesting bits of information about the mysteries of male anatomy from Reggie as well as what a condom was. He wanted to make sure she didn't get pregnant right away – "until they were both ready". Caddy thought it was sweet he loved her enough to wait on a family.

She never once saw her parents or her brothers despite living in the same town. She resumed her lessons with Mr Bunn and spent her lonely days when Reggie was at sea practising her violin and a new guitar he bought for her.

Six months after they were married Reggie was home from a very successful mackerel run off the Dogger Banks and he was in high spirits. They spent the day quite happily in bed, but he was still full of energy and wanted to go out to the pub, something he didn't do often. Nice women didn't go to his fisherman's pubs. Besides, he didn't like her talking to the other men, and he certainly didn't like her talking to his crew. They were too rough, he said, for good girls.

But that night he wanted to go have a drink out with the lads, and he asked her to press his suit, which of course she did. In the pocket of his jacket there was a lump; when she fished inside she found a receipt for Mrs R. Jones' weekly grocery bill in Grimsby and a battered wedding ring.

Standing at the ironing board dressed in her pinny and with a hot iron in her hand, Caddy's world fell apart. She knew what the pain of fear felt like; all her life she had dealt with, lived with, and survived fear, but the gut wrenching grief of betrayal hit her like a freight train. Having your heart smashed was new and the pain – oh the pain was raw. Heartbreak was a physical tearing agony, and she couldn't have hurt more if he had beat her with his fists.

Oh, he was angry, Reggie was, at being caught. He was angry at her for looking in his pocket when she felt the lump. This upset was all her fault, he said. When she screamed at him to get out he was angry at her for getting angry. But Caddy wasn't having any of it. She had lived all her childhood with an angry man who bullied everyone he saw, and she had been out on her own long enough to decide that there were worse things in life than dealing with a raging, cheating, lying man. She had her own fury.

Then he begged. Reggie was getting a divorce. His wife in Grimsby was cold, and he never slept with her. They didn't have a real marriage. Caddy was his true love and if she just was patient –

She kicked him out, slammed the door, and then she sank to the floor and wailed. The physical pain that comes with grief, anger, and the humiliation of betrayal was not the worst part. The dark home of hell was heartbreak .

When Reggie came by the next day she wouldn't listen to his entreaties at all. Caddy pointed out that bigamy was a capital offence with a sentence of seven years in prison. Everyone knew that.

She had a marriage licence where he signed his lie to prove she wasn't just a side piece. He turned pale but accepted it was over and quickly – suspiciously quickly – like he had done this before – offered to pay her expenses for the next six months "while she thought about things".

It turns out if you're married to a bigamist then you're not really married and getting a divorce from him is not necessary.

A week later she was working at Pye's television factory as an assembly line worker. She could walk to work from her nice flat at St. Aubryn's on London Road and by the end of the month she had found another single woman as a flatmate to share expenses. Reggie's six months of household money went into a saving's account.

Caddy

When Caddy was with a man, she enjoyed her time in bed with him. A lot. No man had ever complained about her in bed, although once she had a comment from Ricky that she was a bit too noisy. But that was fair enough at the time; they had three kids in the house and letting your kids know you had a sex life was not something good parents did.

Neptune, though, was a league unto his own. How many women had he been with over the millennia? Uncounted. Yes, the last 3,500 years had been a dry spell, but you never forget how to do it and he had a good memory.

He wasn't interested in her the same way a human man was, at least not the same way as the ones she'd been with. Neptune didn't give a flip about what she looked like. Wrinkles, sags, brown spots, thin hair – none of that bothered him. Anything visual, like naughty underwear or interesting poses, didn't do a thing for him. She found out later that he simply didn't understand pornography. He couldn't understand why a man would masturbate to a porn star's performance any more than he would jerk off to pictures of farm tractors. Neptune wasn't interested in her breasts or kissing her on the mouth and the only reason he bothered with either was simply to get her going.

What turned him on was her smell and she smelled the best when she climaxed. And he made sure she did.

With Neptune Caddy learned the power of pheromones and the overwhelming lust that comes with *musth*. The lord's smell was as intoxicating to her as hers was to him. He snuffled and licked and sucked every inch of her skin like a pig searching for truffles, and the more excited she grew, the more excited he was. But he held back until she was a shuddering moaning mass of jelly because he wanted that smell and when he got it, he finished and was done.

For a while.

When Neptune finally went to sleep, Caddy crawled out of bed and went upstairs to the guest bedroom where she was sleeping and passed out, tired, sore, and feeling very, very good. As big as her normal bed was, Neptune was a very big man and took his half out of the middle, so she left him if only to get a good sleep with what was left of the night.

Caddy

Morning came, and as always Caddy was up very early. She showered, dressed, and was down for breakfast even before that day's housekeeper popped in.

So she made herself a cup of tea and sat down at the kitchen table with the morning paper on her tablet. It was amazing how quickly a person got used to being waited on, she thought, and was about to get up and make her own porridge when an elf popped in.

The housekeepers could be either male or female. Cooking, keeping a house clean and well run wasn't "women's work" like it was for humans, and the idea that a woman could scrub a floor or turn on a washing machine better than a man was laughable. Caddy's needs were handled on a rota managed by Norma, and every day someone new came in. She didn't know that places on the rota were hotly contested and a point of pride for the elves and that they kept a "Lord Cadence Book" of her likes, dislikes, diet, schedules, *etcetera* as if she was a prize racehorse. Which in a way she was.

Today's morning elf was a young woman. She popped in, smiled and waved at Caddy, and then gave her the oddest look. Concerned, Caddy opened her mouth to ask if anything was wrong and the woman squeaked. She literally squeaked, her eyes rolled back in her head, and she popped out.

"Goodness! What's wrong with her?" And Caddy yelled for Norma. Norma didn't come, but Tony did.

"Tony! What happened? Is she okay?"

Tony took a delicate sniff and turned bright red. "No worries, Ms Caddy. Just give us a minute, and we'll be okay. She's fine. Just had a spell."

He popped out, and immediately four male housekeepers popped in. Two of them threw open the windows and went to work wiping down every surface, and the other two started on making the lord's breakfast. Unknown to Caddy, other crews were in the bedrooms changing sheets and cleaning every surface, and hustling Neptune into the shower.

He walked down, damp and grumpy, but he grinned when he saw Caddy.

"Good morning, my love! You're up early! Do you want to –"

"I'm having breakfast, Neptune. Aren't you hungry?"

He nodded, and waved to the cooks who were already piling food in front of them.

"Yes, you're right, as always. I could eat a whale if whales were edible." He tucked in and after a few minutes he looked up and winked. "We have all day, anyway."

"You have all day. My day is scheduled. I'm going to practise on my violin this morning, eat a good lunch, take a nap, eat dinner, and nap again until tonight. We're still going to see if I can wake up some merfolk tonight aren't we?"

The slightest of shadows crossed Neptune's face, but whatever disappointment he had due to her schedule was quickly set aside. Caddy, again, was right. His merfolk were much more important than some play time – which would come again soon enough.

Neptune looked at her closely as she ate. He would have to be careful he didn't hurt her or wear her out. When she was quiet it was obvious she wasn't anywhere near full health even though she was slowly getting better. He desperately needed her to be healthy and strong. Everyone did.

Six months experience with being a lord. Six months of painstaking abilities practise just to move some feathers and now she had the balance of the entire world on her shoulders.

Neptune couldn't imagine what that was like. Every day his joy at discovering another lord and elves was tempered with the new knowledge of how precarious their place in this new world was. He had no idea how many years he had lived on this Earth, but in all those years he had never felt one thing and every day Caddy embodied that one trait he never felt before, and now he did. It was hard to come to terms with it. It wasn't love. It wasn't empathy. It wasn't fear, lust, joy, or loneliness. It was responsibility.

He would finish his breakfast and then do the bowl thing for a while. He was getting better at it and could transfer much larger balls of water now. He wondered if he could learn to do two at one time. If Caddy could set aside her own desires to give her best for his merfolk the least Neptune could do was get healthier and stronger, too.

Caddy

Vernon and Thomas ported to the spot of beach they found on Google Maps, looked it over from their security perspective, and declared it passable.

No place outside of the Rum Lot offices would ever make them happy, but they agreed the risk was not horrible and was certainly less risky than South Beach.

Caddy spent the morning studying which sounds would pass through the water the best, and it was the deep notes that worked the best. Sound waves under 10 hertz would penetrate the sea bed and Extremely Low Frequency, ironically contracted to ELF, was even better. So the lower she could go, the better. Hitting those notes long enough to carry her message, though, would be
hard, hard, hard.

The music she chose would not in itself have those frequencies but would act as a slingshot for the actual sounds much the same way a pitcher winds up before he throws a ball. A wind-up was not a throw, but it sets up the throw and sends the ball on its way.

No one on shore would hear the call. She sighed and hoped that the merfolk would. If not, she was going to wake up some North Sea whales and a few elephants in local zoos,
and that's about it.

Caddy

One o'clock in the morning came, and a few elves ported themselves and Caddy down to the beach with Neptune and most of the soldier elves on the low cliff above. The beach was all shingle, and the waves crashed in, loud and strong. Caddy hesitated. When she had awakened Neptune she was in the water, so she wanted to get in the water again at least to her ankles, but these waves would drag her out to sea.

"Caddy! Wait!"

She heard him, but she couldn't see Neptune high on the cliff. Then she saw two bright points of blue and around her the waves quieted. She wondered how long he could keep the sea quieted, but she wasn't going to ask. So instead she started her song.

When she roused Neptune she was calling the sea and since Neptune *is* the sea, he woke up.

Now she called the merfolk.

She started slow, a gentle awakening, and with each low note she added and amplified with her own magical ability. The song cajoled, insisted, commanded; and with each note the vibrations became deeper and stronger. Her eyes glowed and a soft green light covered her body. The elves on the shingle could feel the vibrations under their feet; the vibrations dislodged bits of sand and pebbles and they slid down the cliff face.

Wake! Wake! It's time!

Faster, deeper, stronger she played. The sea began to ripple, and waves emitted from her not to her.

Come to me!
Come to me!
COME TO ME!

The earth trembled and the elves and Neptune on the clifftop could feel it now. About a hundred metres north, toward Pakefield, the soft cliff gave way, and chunks of hard rocky sand and trees tumbled onto the beach.

Caddy pushed; she pushed as hard as she could. No one could see her body in her bright green glow and around her legs the salty water boiled and churned.

She gave one last crescendo, one last push from deep inside her, and the ground rumbled and shook, and the cliff above her sagged. She ended the song with one achingly long note and put down her bow, finished, utterly spent, and the water around her ankles boiled and steamed. She turned and at that instant an elf dived at her, and she found herself in her sitting room, the smell of burning wood floating up from where her bare feet touched the wood floor.

In the starless night, the sandy cliff from Kessingland to Pakefield crashed into the sea, but no one was there to see it.

Caddy

Caddy collapsed in a heap in the sitting room and Neptune carried her to the guest room bed. Elves would have been forced to wait for her to cool down so they wouldn't get burnt, but he was a lord and her heat didn't bother him.

The elves shooed him out; they could take care of her from that point and he knew they would, but he still came up to check on her every couple of hours. He felt responsible.

Caddy slept for two solid days. She only woke to eat, drink, and stagger to the toilet.

At the end of the second day, when it was full dark and after Neptune finished watching Attenborough's Blue Planet for the third time, he walked up the stairs but went to the top floor first to check on Caddy before he went to his own bed.

He softly knocked on the door, because that's what Caddy always did, and peeked in. There was no elf nurse sitting in the corner anymore. The dangerous period of exhaustion was over, and the lord was just sleeping; she didn't need to be watched.

The room was dark, and Caddy was just a formless black shape huddled under the blankets. All he could see was a lock of white hair, her ear, and a small section of her neck. It was just too tempting; he bent down and nuzzled, inhaling deeply.

"Neptune, that had better be you."

He grinned. "No, it's not me. It's someone else."

"Oh, good, I like a little variety." And she turned to him, her green eyes glittering, and he had the pleasure of making her a very happy woman.

Morning came, and Caddy trotted down the stairs to get her breakfast. She felt great. An elf was cooking kippers and fried potatoes, and it smelled absolutely divine. She didn't know it, but a team of male elves were already up in her room stripping the bed and wiping down the wood.

She was starting on her second kipper when a teenage boy elf popped in, breathless. The elves didn't allow their children to come near her, and this boy was probably at the young end of what they would permit.

He was, as they said when she lived in Texas, as cute as a button, and bowed very low, then just silently stood there, but so excited he was trembling.

"What's up?"

"Lord Cadence," and his eyes got very wide, "there are mermaids down by the Claremont Pier. Two of them. I was sent to tell you."

Caddy had a sharp intake of breath.

"Have you told Lord Neptune?"

"No, ma'am. I was told to tell you first and you would take it from there. I'm not allowed to go near him."

She jumped up, ran to the door, and then stopped.

"Ralph! Do something nice for this boy. What's your name, boy?"

"Louis, ma'am."

"Thank you, Louis! You did a brilliant job."

Caddy ran up the stairs, screaming for Neptune. He was still sound asleep, but she burst into the bedroom and shook him, hard.

"Wake up you big lunk! Wake up!"

Grinning, he lazily turned and opened his eyes.

"Good to see such enthusiasm –"

"Oh shut up! Put your kilt on! I'm not going to tell you why until you put your kilt or trousers on."

He rolled his eyes but did as he was told.

"There, woman, I'm now uncomfortable. What are you going to tell me."

"There's two mermaids under the Claremont Pier."

And just as she knew he would, he burst out of the room without a second thought.

There they were, sitting under the Claremont Pier, talking to a couple of elves, just as if this were 3,500 years ago. Only back then they wouldn't have looked so bedraggled and thin.

Without thinking, Neptune ran to them, and they instantly dove in the water. He followed, and the minute he hit seawater his body reacted, and his legs resumed their fishy form from their unnatural split. The hated kilt slid off, and the three of them raced through the shallow shoals to deeper water.

Caddy ran down to the sea and stopped and watched them speed away. This was a joyful reunion she would not be a part of. She stood alone on the beach, shading her eyes against the glare of the rising sun, looking for Neptune in the churning surf. She didn't see him. He was gone.

She sighed. She had expected him to get distracted by the mermaids, but hadn't expected him to just shoot off without a word. The man didn't even say goodbye.

Norma came and stood behind the lord and looked up, worried.

"Are you all right, Ms Caddy?"

"I'm fine, Norma." Her voice broke a little but then became firmer. "He's where he should be. More merfolk will be coming, I'm sure, and he needs to take care of his people. " She turned to her friend. "I'm fine."

Caddy scanned the horizon. The early morning sun glittered on the grey water, but other than a couple of seagulls, there was no life to be seen.

"Could you please make sure there's a watch set on this beach in case more show up and to let me know if anything happens? I doubt they will come here. Neptune will call them to him now." She looked out to sea again. "And if someone can port me home, I would appreciate it."

"Yes, ma'am."

Caddy

Caddy walked into her old bedroom, which had been Neptune's just a half hour ago, flopped on the bed and stared at the ceiling. She took out her phone and set the timer for fifteen minutes. She would allow herself fifteen minutes to feel sorry for herself. It seemed proportional.

The Lord of the Sea, Neptune, had come into her life about two weeks ago. He came, he charmed, he accomplished his goal, which was to get her to wake up his merfolk, and then he left without a good-bye glance. She didn't think he'd come back and if he did it would only be temporary. The land wasn't his place.

If she had feelings for him it didn't matter.

Caddy had no doubt the two mermaids were the tip of the iceberg and many more would come. She had no idea how or where they hibernated, but if two heard her and came back to this world, then many more were out there swimming in the vast sea. Whales call to each other and their voices travel halfway across the world. The merfolk would do the same. Once merfolk knew where the others were they could port, like elves do so it wouldn't take long for them to coalesce as a people again.

The phone chimed and self-pity time was over.

She called Ralph, who was the housekeeping lead for the day, and told him to put any of Neptune's clothes and things in storage and to make the room ready for her again. Not that much had to be done; the elves kept it immaculate and Neptune didn't have any of his own bits and bobs to worry about. But there might be something in the bathroom. Who knows.

Ralph nodded.

"We'll get this place back to normal right away, ma'am. A fresh mattress and pillows, too."

"Oh, no! Absolutely not! I've had that mattress since I moved here from Texas. Ricky and I slept on that mattress. I'm used to it."

"It's very old, ma'am. Very lumpy now."

"Nope, the mattress stays."

"Yes, ma'am."

She looked at the bed and then shrugged. Time to move on and get back to work.

Wendell

Wendell hurt. He hurt all the time. He hurt in places he didn't think were capable of hurting. His toenails hurt. His hair hurt.

Every day he rose at five in the morning and jogged to Fen Park where the small company of Warrior elves practised their fighting skills and exercised. He would exercise with them, then they would show him some new fighting moves and they would work on perfecting them. They always won when they sparred and he always lost.

The Warrior elves were small, only about 104-105 cm tall, and Wendell was 189 cm tall, but that didn't matter at all. It didn't matter that he weighed twice as much. The elves were fast and fought hard. Wendell remembered a quote he heard somewhere from a boxer. He thought it went "as fast as a hummingbird but stings like a bee." These guys weren't bees; they were hornets.

After they were done making his life miserable, which took about an hour and a half, the elves would leave to do whatever it was they did and Victor would show up and give him weapons training – swordsmanship, knife work, close combat stuff. Victor said that soon he would port Wendell out to someplace in the country and they would do more training with long-range weapons like bows and firearms.

The soldiers pretty much ignored him other than to place bets on how fast he'd lose a bout and, of course, making running bets on when he'd give up altogether.

Wendell didn't give up.

He'd go home, nurse his cuts and bruises, go to work at Asda if it was his shift, then go back home and sleep.

His parents didn't know what to make of this new Wendell. This young man was quieter. He ate an enormous amount of food and he slept every free minute. He didn't play video games any more. He didn't spend hours on the internet. He didn't go out cosplaying as an elf with his friends. Their son had lost all interest in the fantasy world that used to obsess him.

He was leaner, harder. His shoulders broadened and his stomach and back had muscles his mother didn't know existed.

One day he walked downstairs shirtless looking for a clean vest and his worried mother asked if he was on steroids. No mum, he said. Just working out in the mornings with some friends.

Then one morning during a practice bout his opponent zigged when he should have zagged, and Wendell caught him and threw him halfway across the park. The elf ported before he could land and hurt himself, but Wendell won that round, and the elves hooted and clapped and congratulated him.

There wasn't enough money in the world to pay Wendell to quit his Ranger training.

Caddy

A few days after Neptune left, Caddy showed up unannounced to a training session at Fen Park. She didn't say anything, just stood off to the side to watch. Of course, every elf and Wendell knew she was there the minute she walked through the park gate, so they were on their best behaviour and certainly didn't want to lose any bouts in front of a lord. Especially *this* lord. She was tough. That orc didn't pop his head off by himself.

When they were done with their exercises she walked up and had a word with each of them, including Wendell; it was mostly just nonsense like asking if they were getting enough to eat, the correct equipment, and so forth. They all said everything was good because if they did actually complain to a lord their seniors would make their lives miserable for a long, long time. Caddy knew that. And they knew she knew that. But that wasn't the point. She cared about each one of them and they felt it.

Then Caddy walked to her office, which was only a few blocks away, and asked Norma to see if Victor could meet with her when he was free.

When Victor came, Caddy asked him to sit and Norma brought them both a coffee. He perched on the chair stiff-backed, uneasy. What was this lord going to ask him to do now?

"Victor, what is your measure of Wendell? Cons first."

He looked at his coffee and took a sip. "Naive, soft, terribly out of shape, doesn't know crap about anything military, needs to take more baths."

"Pros."

"Stubborn, willing to learn, great capacity for pain, doesn't complain, observant."

"Will he make a good Ranger?"

"If I say yes I'll be punishing myself because you'll make me keep him on. If I say no I'll feel guilty because we'll have to cut him loose and that will destroy him."

"You'd only feel guilty because you should have said yes." Caddy tilted her head and smiled at the soldier. "You've surely cut unfit people loose before. I doubt you felt guilty."

He nodded and grimaced. He could see where this was going.

"Victor, you're going to turn this nice soft young man into a Ranger and then we're going to use him to be the core of a company of them. He's your practice Ranger, so to speak. Our guinea pig Ranger to use while we develop this program. The goal will be a hundred elite individuals who will have elf training and support who will then scatter into the population to do whatever it is we need them to do. All human, all working underground to protect elves out there in the community. They will go where elves can't go and do elf work. What do you think of that idea?"

"I hate it, Lord Cadence. Really, I do. Can't think of a worse assignment."

"Will you do it?"

He sighed from the bottom of his hairy, black heart. Of course he would.

Caddy grinned at Victor's dour face and called to her PA. "Norma, could you please have someone fetch Wendell and bring him here?'

Wendell

Wendell wasn't told the full extent of Caddy's Ranger plans. It was still very early days yet and she needed to see him go through more training to prove himself. But he was given an offer to work for RumLot, Ltd. as a full time contract employee for three times minimum wage. He was also issued a really bitchin' elf-designed and elf-made uniform. His only regret was that he was not allowed to tell anyone he was in Ranger training, just that he was working in the Rum Lot stockroom. If he told anyone, anyone at all, he would be fired. They would know.

He was so happy he could have cried.

Wendell went home that night, told his parents he was quitting Asda and working somewhere else and didn't say another word. Between themselves his parents worried that he was selling drugs.

Caddy

A week came and went and Neptune didn't come back. Merfolk were spotted up and down the east coast of Britain and even earned a speculative article in the Daily Mail. Then some were spotted in Greece and a family whose dog fell off their yacht outside of Cadiz swore on Tik Tok that a merman saved the pup from drowning and gave him back. He was renamed Aquadog and his post garnered over a million likes.

Life went on for Caddy; she worked on her plan and talked over aspects of it with Ellen, various clan leaders, and specialists. She consulted with the tech department and with Tony who was managing finance and banking now.

Caddy woke up elves in Laxfield, pushing the southern boundary a bit further south. Ellen and Wendell both came to that re-birthing because Caddy thought it was important that humans who worked for elves understood why they were so vulnerable. It took a while for some of the elves to feel comfortable with a human being there, but if the lord said so, then that's what the lord gets. Besides, it was Ellen and Wendell! It's not like they were outsiders.

Caddy's plan of gradual integration slowly began to work.

The elf population eased into the fabric of Lowestoft life. Elves bought things, which made the merchants happy. They fixed up houses, they purchased and beautifully restored buildings on the High Street, and elf traders opened up market stalls. If the people who worked in the stalls were a bit short that didn't bother the Lowies. The new "people" kept to themselves but were invariably polite, cheerful, and spoke proper Suffolk. Besides, Lowies had had plenty of short people living here before the newcomers showed up.

The same gradual, silent, integration was occurring across Suffolk and a bit into eastern Norfolk. Elves came back and most people didn't notice at all. They were just happy that the economy was picking up and things seemed a bit nicer now.

Ellen worked hard to smooth over any rough patches that popped up between humans and elves and kept a close eye on social media. The elves' computer systems monitored every post, like, and share and quashed or buried most comments about the elves.

Crime decreased in the areas where elves lived, and no one quite knew why. Orcs lived in with the human population and thought they were human, too, but the elves spotted them immediately. When Caddy said it would be nice to track orcs just so elves would know to avoid them, the tech guys took to her idle wish and ran with it. Every orc was located, and without orcs knowing a thing, facial recognition cameras blanketed the area. With a massive bank of computers and AI to sort it all out, elves always knew where each orc was. Great Yarmouth could not happen again, at least not where elves were firmly established.

Caddy was very strict on how they could use that information. Some elves wanted to "take care" of every orc they came across even if they were just garden-variety irritants, but she wouldn't allow it. Balance meant taking the sour with the sweet and as long as the orcs weren't harming elves in any way or doing anything illegal, they had to be left alone. If they stole or assaulted a human a crime report was automatically lodged with the constabulary along with video evidence and human police and courts took care of them. Eventually some areas just became unprofitable for most criminals and the orcs wandered away to find easier places to bother.

That didn't mean the elves didn't take some proactive steps to encourage the worst ones to leave. One particularly horrible town councillor found she was heir to a tiny terrace house in London, but she could only have it if she lived in it. So she moved. She was happy, and half of Lowestoft was even happier.

More and more elves openly lived normal lives in Suffolk and absolutely no one cared.

Neptune

Almost two months after Neptune left he came back.

Caddy was sitting in her office, taking a break from reading a report by Tony titled "Integrating Elf AI with the American Banking System and the Associated Risks with Transferring Funds To and From the UK." Just reading the title put her to sleep.

It had charts.

And an attached PowerPoint presentation.

So she did something productive, which meant practising moving things around the room with her abilities. She was past the feather and bauble stage now and could move pencils fairly easily. Today she was trying to move three at once and was almost there when Norma popped in.

"Ms Caddy!"

The pencils fell to her desk with a clatter and one rolled onto the floor. Caddy glanced up at her PA, irritated, then concerned. The usually unflappable Norma was upset.

"Ms Caddy! Neptune's back. He's on the beach with a bunch of merfolk. He called for an elf to ask you to come down and see him."

Caddy sat back and didn't quite know how to take this announcement. Mixed emotions didn't begin to describe her reaction. Happiness? Sure. Lust? Probably, if she was honest with herself. Irritation at being jerked around? Definitely.

"Okay, Norma. Could you find an elf to port me there?"

"Yes, ma'am. He's already waiting for you." Then she hesitated and cleared her throat. "Ms Caddy, you'll come back, won't you?"

Surprised, Caddy turned to Norma. "Norma, I'll always come back. Why wouldn't
I come back?"

"He's a lord, Ms Caddy." She waved her hands, helpless. "You're a lord –"

"And lords go a-roaming, Norma. Where did I hear that? Someone said it to me once." Caddy smiled. "Norma, I might go a-roaming, but I'll always come back, I promise you. Lowestoft is my home. Elves – all elves – are my clan."

"Yes, Ms Caddy." Norma sniffled, unconvinced. Caddy sighed; the only way she could prove to this elf, and all the elves, that she was their lord and reliable was to go somewhere and come back. The proof, as they say, was in the pudding. Until then, soothing words wouldn't be enough to make them feel better.

Her porting elf was waiting in the hall; Caddy put on her hat and within seconds she was on the beach.

And there was Neptune, Lord of the Seas, fat and happy, and lolling on the hard sand with at least two dozen merfolk. He spotted her immediately and sat up, waving his arms as if she would miss him in the crowd and shouting, "CADDY! CADDY!"

Caddy smiled and trotted up and gave him a big hug and a kiss on the cheek, which was exactly what he wanted.

"Oh, Caddy, I missed you!"

"Did you now!" And she gave him another hug. He didn't notice that she didn't say she missed him. "How've you been? You look wonderful! " She looked at the mermaids and mermen; they were silent and still and stared at her. "And these are your people?"

They didn't move except for the occasional twitch of a flipper. They just stared, unblinking. Neptune took no notice of them at all. He just kept grinning at Caddy.

Norma popped in behind her, and suddenly a bunch of elves brought a beach chair for Caddy to sit on along with huge hampers of food and drink, which loosened up the merfolk. Who doesn't like a beach party?

So Caddy wasted the afternoon on the beach, and Neptune told her what he did since the day the first mermaids came by. Those two were, as Caddy guessed, just the vanguard. The merfolk's hibernation wasn't like the elves, where they went to some in-between place and were reborn in eggs. Merfolk escaped to hibernate in huge deep water caverns under the Arctic where the extreme cold and deep pressure put them in a catatonic state much like what Neptune did. Like toads that can be frozen indefinitely and then return to life with the spring thaw, merfolk just went into a frozen suspended animation state and waited for a wake up call.

Unlike the elves, which were almost killed off by the human/orc genocide, merfolk escaped most of that persecution, so almost all of the Before Times population was returning. Neptune knew that millions had awakened, but under the Antarctic ice shelves and in some very very deep mid-Atlantic trenches he suspected that some were still hiding. Like the elves who looked for their own to wake up, the merfolk were searching the corners and crevasses of the undersea world to make sure no remaining mermaids and mermen were still sleeping.

In the meantime, Neptune was taking Caddy's example of laying low and keeping his people as far away from humans and orcs as possible. It wasn't too hard; the sea was vast and there were millions of miles of uninhabited shorelines to visit when the open seas became tiring.

"It seems that everything is working out for you, Neptune." Caddy leaned toward the lord, not an easy thing to do in a low collapsible beach chair, and patted him on the arm. "I'm so happy for you."

He took a drink of the very good wine the elves gave him. "It's all because of you, Caddy. I can't tell you how grateful I am. I'll always be in your debt.

"That's one reason I came back – to say thank you. And to apologise for leaving you without a word." Neptune looked sheepish. "I know that was an arsehole thing to do, but when I got to the middle of the channel there were untold thousands – I can't tell you how many – merfolk milling in the water. All around were those damnable human metal ships, and I had to gather up my people and lead them out to safer waters. One thing led to another, and suddenly I realised that I'd been away for a week."

Caddy nodded. "Then another one thing led to another one thing, and it was two weeks, and so on."

"Yeah, but I'm back now!" And he grinned at her, happy she understood.

Caddy leaned back in the chair and looked at the sea, her face expressionless. Then she turned and smiled.

"And how long do you and your folk plan to stay? I know the Channel isn't the type of water you like."

Neptune grimaced. "It stinks, and there's all sorts of rubbish in it." He took another big gulp of the wine. "I want to ask if you'll come to visit me. I've found an island in the tropics. It's beautiful and warm." He looked at her, pleading. "Come stay a week with me, and we'll talk and have a good time. Please, it'll be fun!"

Caddy was taken aback. She had talked about roaming with Norma but didn't really expect to actually go somewhere.

"Oh, I don't know, Neptune. I can't swim to the tropics!"

"No, no! You don't have to swim! The merfolk will port you. Merfolk don't have *terrior.* Sea water isn't like dirt; it covers the earth and flows around. They can port you anywhere as long as it's in salt water. You'll be ported there and ported back. You'll just be wet at both ends. They can't port on land."

"So you promise that I will be able to come back anytime I want?"

"Of course. I won't hold you." He looked offended at the thought. "You're a lord. I don't think I could if I wanted to."

"I would make your life miserable, you big lunk."

She didn't say no, so she was saying yes. With that Neptune laughed and said, yes, he knew she would make his life a living hell if he made it hard for her to come back. Of course, his plan was to make her life so happy she wouldn't want to come back, but he didn't say that aloud.

"My elves will be upset. I don't know how they'll react so I'm not going to promise anything now, but I will tell you tomorrow one way or the other."

Neptune was not the least bit worried about land elves. They would do whatever Caddy said, and they had no power to keep her, so he gave her a hug and a snuffle on her neck, just to remind her what she would be missing and let her go home, well pleased with how it all went.

Neptune had no doubt that when he returned to his island Caddy would return with him.

Caddy

Norma cried, Tony looked crestfallen, and the rest of her elves were so upset she almost gave up on the entire idea. Ellen didn't know what to think.

"You won't come back!" Norma wailed.

"Of course, I'll come back! I have his word that I can come back anytime I want. They will port me." Caddy was getting irritated. This emotional outpouring was excessive. It was un-British. And not a little insulting; didn't she already promise Norma she would never leave them?

Ellen was a little more measured, but Caddy could tell she was worried.

"Let's say he doesn't. What if he just leaves you on the island and tells the merfolk to go away? He doesn't have to put you in a cage."

Caddy raised an eyebrow. She hadn't thought of that. Then Tony pulled out his phone. Even in an emergency meeting he checked the world stock exchanges and Caddy knew the solution.

"Norma, I'm going to take my phone with me. You know it has a tracker in it. You can trace me anywhere in the world. For that matter, you can put trackers in my luggage."

"You're taking luggage?"

"Why not? I'm going on holiday! Those merfolk were all as naked as newborn babies. I don't think they know the concept of clothes and I don't want to spend a week with sand up my arse."

She turned back to Norma. "If you and the tech guys can track me there's no place in the world you can't send a helicopter to if I need to be picked up. I don't think the merfolk can deal with anything coming from the sky. You can make a backup rescue plan."

"Can't you just bonk him here?" Tony blurted out.

"I *beg* your pardon!"

"Sorry, I don't mean to intrude –"

"Too late."

" – but it seems such a waste. If you do it here we can at least get some good out of it."

Caddy gaped at the elf, open-mouthed.

"*Were you watching me and Neptune?*"

"No, no – nothing like that. It's the Scent. We have a lot of women now and they need it."

The lord leaned back in her chair and her next words were quiet and dangerous.

"I am obviously missing something here. Please go back to the beginning and explain."

Caddy's eyes glowed.

All the elves popped out of the room except for Norma, who was still sniffling, and Tony, who now had no fear of her.

"Ms Caddy, we elves take care of lords; you know that. Didn't you ever wonder
why we do that?

Caddy furrowed her brow. "I thought you needed my protection. And to wake
up other elves."

"But not historically," Tony continued. "For untold years we didn't have enemies that lords needed to protect us from. Orcs and humans were under control. We didn't need lords to wake us up. We had alarm clocks for that. So why would elves put up with abusive, snotty, selfish lords?"

Caddy raised an eyebrow. Why, indeed?

Tony took a deep breath and just spit it out. "Because the only way an elf woman can get pregnant is to drop an egg into her womb and get it fertilised by a willing male. Just like humans, orcs, and lords. But the only way to release that elf egg is to start a hormone cascade."

"Just like humans." Caddy was beginning to get an inkling of where this was going.

Tony continued. "But elf women don't go on monthly cycles. Their ovulation is started by pheromones. They have to have the right smell – the Scent. No Scent, no egg. No egg, no baby. Lords and elves are symbiotic, pheromone-driven tribes."

He took a big breath.

"The only person who can make the Scent is a female lord. And you are the ONLY female lord we know of. Men are useless –"

"I know that." Caddy couldn't help herself; she smiled.

"The male lords can't make it," Tony corrected himself. "But they're one way to make the female lords climax and when they sweat their hormones make the Scent. So we need happy female lords. We really don't need male lords at all. But if we lose you we lose the ability of our entire race to make babies. No babies and we will go extinct."

Caddy leaned back and looked at the ceiling. She took a deep breath.

"So that housekeeper –"

"You came down for breakfast and the house reeked. She took one whiff of you after your night with Neptune and her hormones went wild. She ported home and her bond-man contributed his bit and now she's pregnant. She's hysterically happy."

Norma nodded. "Due right after the first of the year."

"But I don't see female elves running around –"

Norma sniffled. "Oh we used to just go up and give the female lords a big hug and sniff their crotches, but we decided you wouldn't like that."

"Thanks. You thought right." Caddy had to smile again.

"So now we take your sheets and cut them up into little squares and package them in sealed plastic bags and sell them in our chemist shop in Safe Haven. Same with the rags we used to clean up and de-scent the rooms, but they go for a discount."

Caddy leaned forward and put her face in her hands, and her shoulders started to shake. Ellen leaned forward and stroked her head. "Ms Caddy, don't cry –"

But Caddy wasn't crying; she was laughing so hard she couldn't breathe.

"You… you… are cutting uuu-up my dirty sheets…" Then she looked at Ellen and went back into gales of air-gulping laughter. Ellen giggled and started to laugh, and then she was crying, too.

The two elves looked at each other. They didn't see the humour.

"Ms Caddy. This is serious –"

"Oh! Oh! My sides hurt!" Tears were streaming down both Caddy and Ellen's faces.

It took ten minutes for Caddy and Ellen to get under control. Every time they settled down one would say something about "popping one's cork" or "coming around the mountain" or "three sheets to the wind" or something equally stupid, and it would set them off again.

Finally Caddy settled down, and after wiping her eyes and giggling she had
come to a decision.

"I'm going to go on a little holiday. I'll be gone for seven days. Norma is going to get the techies to wire me and my bags up all to hell and I'm going to be tracked. I am absolutely sure I'm going to be safe against orcs and there will be no humans around if only because Neptune doesn't want them either. If I don't come back by midnight of day seven you can send in the marines or whoever you decide to hire to go pick me up." Caddy sighed.

"Are there any questions? No? Okay then. Go now and have a good night's sleep." Caddy waved them away, "And Norma, please buy me a couple of small watertight suitcases and pack one with as many beach towels as you can get in there. I will endeavour to bring back a souvenir or two. No promises."

The elves ported themselves and Ellen out, and Caddy was left sitting alone in her sitting room, shaking her head.

"What I do for these guys

Caddy and Neptune

The next morning Caddy told Neptune she would come visit for seven days, but she couldn't leave until the next day because she had things to tend to. She also explained she would have her phone with her in case of any emergencies back in Lowestoft and she would need someone nearby who would be around to port her back if needed. He shrugged and agreed readily enough. He didn't understand why she would want to come shooting back if she was having a good time, but that was the "responsibility" thing again.

Caddy was back and forth between the beach and the shop offices all day. Norma bought two small watertight suitcases; they were modified according to the techies instructions and inside one was a bunch of beachwear and Caddy's hats, and inside the other was a bundle of beach towels. Unexpectedly, Victor came by with an elf knife in an arm sheath, and Caddy put it on and thanked him.

She was ready.

Ready for her first holiday in years – decades! – Caddy stood on the shoreline dressed in a wetsuit, bags at her side, and a small waterproof backpack on. She felt rather ridiculous next to the nude merfolk, but she wasn't going to prance around South Beach naked no matter what the others thought.

Actually, she felt naked without her hat, but that was another issue.

"So how do we do this?" She cocked her head at Neptune.

Uncharacteristically, he was nervous. He wanted everything to go right and in the water Caddy was as delicate as sea foam. She wasn't like the merfolk who could just speed out to deep water like dolphins and port from there.

"I"m going to carry you to deep water. Porting in shallow water is a bit more difficult. It can be done, but it's not as smooth. When we get to deep water, Ser, (and he nodded to a merman) is going to make a port and just like on land, you go through."

Neptune gave a push with his muscular fin, and when he was out in the deeper water he turned and held out his arms. "C'mon, Caddy!" She hesitated.

"What about my bags?"

"Don't worry about your bags; they'll get them. They'll probably be there before you."

She heaved a big sigh and waded in.

"Y'know, I haven't been swimming in the sea for almost 50 years. I walk by the sea, I don't swim in it." And then she was in his arms, and he laughed.

"You don't know what you're missing then!"
Neptune rubbed his face in her hair. "I forgot how small
you are!" And he turned and headed out to sea.

Caddy didn't think anyone had ever called her
small, but compared to Neptune – or even the average
merman – she guessed she was. Neptune was huge on land.
In the sea, with his tail, he was at least a metre longer. He
carried Caddy in his arms to the shoals, and that was like
being on a jet ski. But once they were there a merman
swam up with a harness, and they strapped it on Neptune.
She was told to get up in that, which freed up his arms, and
then he really picked up speed. Speeding through the water
on the back of the Lord of the Seas was, to put it mildly,
exhilarating. When he realised that Caddy was not afraid
and was even enjoying the ride, he played around a bit,
making big unnecessary loops and even circling a sailboat
with a very startled crew.

Caddy waved.

Soon they were in deep water and Neptune stopped.

"Ser is going to make the port. It's underwater, so
you have to dive. You'll only be underwater for less than a
minute. Are you going to be okay with that?"

"Bit late to ask!" Caddy rolled her eyes. "I'll manage. Just point me the right way so I don't get lost."

"Oh, we'll go through together. You won't get lost. Take a deep breath!"

Caddy took a huge breath, and immediately she was underwater. She tried hard to keep her eyes open and vowed next time to bring goggles, but she doubted if she could see any more with them. The water was murky and very cold, and the currents pushed hard. She spotted a very faint circle and Neptune shot through it with a single powerful swipe of his tail. Suddenly the murky cold water was clear and warm, and Caddy could see the bright sun above her shining through tranquil seas.

They broke the surface and she gulped air, and that was that. Easy peasy.

Norma

Norma watched the FindMyPhone icon that represented Caddy disappear from the map on the big screen in the conference room. Everyone in the room held their breath.

Nothing.

Then the two icons that represented her bags disappeared.

Nothing.

Suddenly the map wildly twirled as it reset to the new location. All three icons popped up on the tiny island of Santo Antonio of São Tomé and Príncipe, in the Gulf of Guinea, off the west coast of Africa. Caddy and the bags were in a nature reserve that took up the south half of the island.

The group let out a collective breath, and then they went to work.

"At least," Ellen said, "she didn't lose her luggage. It's always a hassle when that happens."

———————————————————

Caddy

Caddy landed on the beach like Botticelli's Venus, although in a wetsuit and without the great hair.

Not that her fine hair mattered; she and Neptune were the only people with hair. Not a single merfolk hair to share between the lot of them. And there were a lot of them.

Tens of thousands of merfolk, it seemed, had taken over the island. Looking down the beach the scene reminded Caddy of those nature documentaries showing masses of seals crowding huge beaches. Or maybe Brighton Beach during summer holidays. Only instead of seals or sunburnt Brits this sunbaked beach was cheek-to-jowl with lounging, chattering, gambling, screaming, drinking, gossiping, eating, sleeping merfolk. Many thousands more heads, tails, and torsos dotted the sea and Caddy suspected that under the water it was equally crowded.

"Look at them, Caddy! Aren't they beautiful!" Neptune was so happy and proud of them that Caddy had to smile and agree. No one could say that merfolk weren't beautiful in their own (slightly creepy) way.

The average merman was a massive two and a half metres long. They were about one-third humanoid on the top and two-thirds mammalian fish on the bottom. All merfolk were countershaded, so their backs were very dark and their fronts very light. Most were spotted and the colours varied from whites to browns to greys and black.

Their hairless heads were gently bullet shaped, with large round eyes, small pointed elf ears, and an almost lipless slash of a mouth. They looked like humans, but not.

The women were smaller, but not by much. They were finer-boned and their breasts were non-existent. Like the men they were counter-shaded, but their fins sparkled with bright splashes of colour on the edges as if they had been dipped in paint. They wore strands and strands of jewellery – necklaces, bangles, and headbands. If it sparkled and existed to be worn, they wore it.

Like wolves and chihuahuas who were of the same tribe, it was hard to believe that the elves, who looked exactly like lords only small, were the same tribe as merfolk who looked so other-worldly and were huge.

As she walked up the beach the merfolk turned and stared at Caddy with open and occasionally hostile curiosity. Neptune swam parallel with the shore and led her to a rocky outcropping where he hauled up out of the water like an Olympic swimmer out of the pool. Behind them was a private courtyard of sand bordered with palms for shade and flowering bushes for colour.

It was really very pretty, and despite the crowds further down the beach it was quiet and sheltered. In a corner of the sandy space someone had pitched a canvas cabana that had "Sandals" written on it, and there were pillows piled in front. Inside the tent, Caddy saw her two bags.

"This is very pretty, Neptune. Is this where you live?" Caddy examined every aspect of the shelter.

"I live mostly in the sea, but if I want to come on land, this is one of the places I come to. I have homes like this all over the world, so it really depends on where I am." He looked at her closely. "Do you like it?"

"On a beautiful day like this it's charming. I suppose that on foul days you have some place to take shelter."

"We can –"

"I think I would very much like to get out of this wetsuit. It's really made to protect me from the North Sea and here it's very uncomfortable. While I'm doing that could we have some food and drink? I'm very thirsty."

Neptune smiled and turned to his staff, and Caddy went to her bags and opened them up. Norma had packed a variety of swimsuits, cover ups, and shorts and tops. Caddy thought about a swimsuit and rejected it for now. She took out a loose white cotton cover up, threw it over her naked body, and stuck a straw hat on. That would keep her from burning to a crisp, she thought. She wondered if Norma had remembered sunscreen.

When she went back out there was a nice picnic spread on blankets, and Caddy noted that it wasn't all fish, just mostly fish. There was a bit of fruit and on a tray in the middle, a pile of Snickers bars. Neptune was lolling on one side, and there were about ten other merfolk sitting around busily eating and drinking and chatting in their accented elvish.

They went quiet when Caddy came out. Neptune called her to come sit by him and he patted the ground next to him.

"This is Ser, who you met; Jen –," and he quickly went around the room pointing and naming. "And, my friends, this is Lord Cadence."

They nodded and a couple smiled, but most just looked at her blankly.

"Lord Neptune, she doesn't look like a lord. She looks like a human. Are you sure?" This was spoken by a beautiful woman on Neptune's left. She had iridescent purple markings on her fins and her torso was draped in pearl necklaces. She also wore a sneer which didn't add to her attractiveness.

There was a collective intake of breath and Caddy was stunned at her discourtesy. So was Neptune who turned bright red and hissed, "Leave." But Caddy held up her hand and said, "No, wait." Which caused another stir among the merfolk. This woman had just said "no" to Lord Neptune, and he didn't lash out at her. Two merfolk in the back popped away.

All eyes were on Caddy who looked very grave. Then she smiled and looked the purple-finned woman in the eye. She flicked a finger, and two grapes jumped from the platter to her hand and her eyes glowed bright. She cocked her head and said, "What I *am* is a guest of Lord Neptune. I think that deserves some courtesy." She ate a grape. "But I am curious as to why you think Lord Neptune is such a fool. What does a lord look like to you?"

Neptune was furious, but he said nothing. This was Caddy's show. His fluke twitched.

Someone in the back giggled. And it wasn't at
Caddy. The woman's eyes darted around the room; there
was nothing she could say to worm her way out of her
horrible gaffe. But she tried.

"I didn't say Lord Neptune was a fool. Naturally, he
isn't fooled by anyone. I –" And she stuttered; this was
getting worse and worse. "I apologise if that was the
impression I gave." And she bowed to Neptune and smiled
prettily. He didn't smile back.

Not good enough, thought Caddy. This was a bully
who felt she needed to put Caddy in her place. She didn't
apologise to Caddy, not at all. This was a dominance play,
pure and simple. Mean girl stuff. Neptune's lover? A court
favourite who felt threatened?

"You didn't answer my question. Answer it."
Caddy's eyes glowed bright now. A flash of green like the
northern lights traced across her face. She ate another
grape. "Don't leave
until you do."

"I ... I thought lords were –" Fear was setting in. Oh, shit, this ugly little woman really was a lord. And she was angry! What would this lord do to her? What would Neptune do to her for being so rude to his guest? And now, somehow, her words were seen as an insult to him, too. It was obvious to everyone she longed to escape and port out, but now she had a direct order from a lord to stay. The mermaid swallowed, her mouth suddenly dry.

" – taller."

A couple in the back snickered at Purple Fin's weak answer. Caddy grinned and turned to Neptune and winked.

"So lords here are measured by the inch? If I stood on a rock would that help?"

The tension broke, and everyone laughed. Purple Fin looked like she was going to cry and wanted to be anywhere in the world but here, but she hadn't been given permission to leave yet.

"You *are* short," Neptune said and raised his hand as if to measure her height. He was still furious, but the moment for lashing out had passed.

Caddy turned to Purple Fin and simply said, "Go." And the mermaid popped out instantly. Everyone immediately relaxed.

"Neptune, that rude woman made everyone's name just fly from my head. Could you please introduce me to these lovely people again? Only slower please?" So they started over from the beginning, and everyone who had stayed was formally introduced again to the lord. They all bowed and smiled and said nice things.

―――――――――――――――――――

Caddy

It didn't take long for Caddy's encounter with the rude courtier to pass down the gossip chain. She had levitated two grapes which stretched her abilities to their limit, but by the time the story made it to the end of the beach she had juggled boulders and burned like a bonfire.

What she didn't know was that, really, the merfolk didn't have much to do with lords because Neptune didn't. In Before Times, lords, weak or strong, didn't often visit their watery world.

If Neptune was in a gaming or carousing mood he would go on land to visit friendly lords alone. If a mermaid chanced on a lord walking on a beach, which was an incredibly rare event in itself, she would immediately port away and, of course, most lords couldn't follow her. Elves could only go to sea about twenty miles from shore which left vast expenses of open water exclusively for the use of the merfolk.

If the merfolk had thought it through they probably could have survived the human/orc wars, but they were creatures who schooled and when some of them panicked and fled they all followed blindly. Caddy found the occasional clever one, but, as a whole, they weren't too bright a species. Not like their elven cousins. Not at all.

The first two days passed with visits to pretty parts of the island, raucous meals with Neptune's court, and frequent "naps" in the cabana, which always ended up with Caddy carefully folding one of Norma's towels and packing it away in a plastic zip bag.

Their naps were a lot of fun, but they quickly discovered that Neptune's bulk made him too heavy to easily move around while on land.

Now that he was back in full health, he was bigger in every way – more muscled, broader, and much taller than he was when he was in Lowestoft.

Neptune was made for the sea, not the land. His fishing tackle (not to put too fine a point on it) was proportioned for a larger female than Caddy. For the first time in her life Caddy was too petite for a man to mount and she found that extremely amusing. It never occurred to her before that all of the men she bedded (and there were only three before Neptune) had been rather small-framed humans. When Neptune had a human lower half he fit. Now he didn't.

She wasn't bothered; there were lots of ways to have fun in bed, and Neptune made sure she was happy and sweating her intoxicating scent which he couldn't get enough of.

But at the end of the second day he started to hint that she could make a little change. Would Caddy consider morphing? Just for a few days? He could turn into a man, but that would knock him out for at least a day now and he had a lot of duties with managing his merfolk. If she could turn into a mermaid, just for a day or so, she could visit the ocean depths with him, too.

C'mon, he said, it'll be fun.

Caddy had no idea how to do that. She didn't even know where to start.

"You didn't know how to move something with your mind until you did it. You didn't know how to sing with your magical abilities until you did it. Lords can morph and you, I think, are a powerful lord. You can do this."

For the first time, Neptune lied to Caddy. He lied by omission. He didn't mention the dangers of morphing. He didn't talk about the pain involved with breaking and rearranging bones and flesh.

Every action has an equal and opposite reaction. Balance will be served. Morphing takes energy, like anything else, and there would be a cost. He didn't talk about that bit.

Nor did Neptune talk about weaker lords who morphed and never went back to their normal form, imprisoned and doomed in their new bodies.

If Caddy morphed into a mermaid and couldn't go back to her birth form, would that be so bad?

He did warn her that she needed to keep about the same or more mass. If she morphed to something very small she might not have the brain power to remember who she was, and she wouldn't know to go back.

"So I shouldn't morph into a worm, then."

"Exactly. Keep focussed on large intelligent creatures. Turn into a dolphin, not a gerbil."

Caddy was intrigued. Neptune switched back and forth at will and didn't seem to show any ill effects other than being tired. He was very weak from his long sleep when he first changed to a full man during that stormy night in Lowestoft, so that explained his extreme exhaustion and the need to take a few days to recover. But when he went back to his merman form it was instantaneous. She saw that for herself. Caddy, on the other hand, was pretty strong now. She felt healthy. Did she have the reserves inside to do this?

Caddy didn't say no, so Neptune pushed and wheedled and teased and kissed her, and by the morning of the third day she threw up her hands and agreed to try.

Gleeful in victory, Neptune wasn't going to let Caddy change her mind and had them both immediately ported to an isolated cove.

"You've thought this through, haven't you? You've been planning this!" Caddy didn't know if she was amused or annoyed.

"Of course, I have. I want your first time to be a good one." Neptune's eyes glowed blue, and he tenderly stroked the side of her face. "Just do what I tell you to do; relax and just – flow –"

Neptune swam with Caddy to deep water. She was naked, so no clothes to constrict or bind as she changed and she floated vertically in the warm water while Neptune floated in front of her, holding her hands out. They looked like they were about to dance.

Neptune's deep deep voice rumbled soothingly, calmly, safely, and Caddy knew he was trying to put her in a meditative, hypnotic frame of mind. He methodically worked to get her concentrating totally on this change.

She smiled, the glow came to her eyes, and he smiled back. Trusting, loving, she let him guide her. Caddy allowed herself to change.

"Relax. You don't feel anything outside of your body. Think about your body. Think about your head, your arms, your fingers – think about what you want to become."

Neptune's voice faded. She was inside herself, thinking about nothing but her body and –

Caddy's head snapped back and her eyes rolled.

Her body burst with a green fire that burned Neptune's hands where he was holding on to hers; he didn't let go, but damn, it scared him. He had never done this before, another detail he had neglected to tell Caddy, and this violent reaction was a complete shock to him. He didn't know if someone had trained him to morph, but if someone had it was so far back in the distant past that even such an intense memory was lost to time. He just had enough whispers of memory of watching other lords morph to give it a go with Caddy.

She screamed in pain and shuddered and he still didn't let go. If he released her to the water he was afraid she would drown.

The pain was mind-numbing and she couldn't move. Caddy could barely breathe through the tears that ran down her face. It hurt. It hurt. It hurt so bad. And then when she thought she couldn't take another minute of it, the tidal wave of pain ebbed to a bad memory, and it was over, leaving her shaken and exhausted.

And a mermaid.

"Caddy! Speak! Are you all right?" Neptune was still holding Caddy's hands tight.

She gulped for air like a runner after an Olympic sprint, but she felt good; good but different.

Caddy looked into Neptune's eyes, confused, and then back down to her feet. But she had no feet or legs. Her lower half was a sleek body with massive flukes. She wasn't countershaded like the merfolk; her flukes were an iridescent green that faded to bright blue streaks that in turn faded into her human body. Her hands were webbed, but north of her belly button that was all that she could see as changed.

Neptune was stunned then ecstatic.

"By gods, Caddy, you're beautiful! Look at this colour! Look at your tail!" He dove down to examine her and felt her with his hands. She tried to bat him away and in doing so sank under the water – and she realised she could breathe! She didn't fill her lungs with sea water, but gills appeared under her ribcage, a froth of lace-like gills that grabbed oxygen from the water. Neptune was delighted with those, too, and tickled them.

They spent the rest of the day swimming and exploring both the underwater world and her new body, which was beautiful and worked well in every way.

On the fourth day Caddy and Neptune swam to deep water. He showed her how the dolphins corralled and caught fish for the merfolk. He brought her an octopus to play with, and she was able to have a conversation with it. She sang for the dolphins and whales, and they sang back, the high pings of the dolphins and the low rumbles of the whales spanning impossible octaves.

He showed her how to body surf!

That night, the merfolk had a wild party on the beach. Caddy had never been to anything like it, but then she hadn't been to many wild parties in her life. None, in fact. The mermaids danced in the water, the mermen sang, and everyone laughed and cried and got roaring drunk.

The party went on until late in the night when, at some unknown signal, mermaids slipped into the sea and formed a circle out in the deep warm water. Caddy was alone, Neptune had gone off somewhere, so she floated out to watch the mermaids dance, but this wasn't a dance; it was a mating ball. Unlike the land elves, they didn't use a scent to trigger their fertility. Scents were for lords and land elves and to a lesser extent humans. But not for merfolk because the sea diffused the pheromones. What merfolk did was form a mating ball.

The mermaids danced a circle and sang to lure in the men (who didn't need much luring). The dancing couples swirled faster and faster, and the circle became tighter and tighter until they formed a wriggling mass of arms, fins, long eel-like penises, and after a few minutes of the orgy, the sea was milky with sperm. Then they split off into twos and threes and finished their copulation.

Caddy turned to go back to the beach, and as she passed through a cluster of mating couples there was Neptune banging away with the snotty mermaid who doubted Caddy was a lord. Neither of them saw her; they were too involved in what they were doing.

Caddy turned away and went back to the beach. Later, when Neptune returned to the party, she was already back in the cabana, curled into a tight ball, sleeping. He didn't wake her up. He didn't need to.

Morning found Neptune stretching out on the beach catching the sun while Caddy lounged a few feet away in the shadows.

She wasn't going to risk a sunburn, she said.

He was quite happy with how things were going. His merfolk played and quarrelled in the cove, their musical voices chattering in the distance. Children giggled and mothers fretted over them. There were plenty of fish to feast on.

Everything was as it should be.

He said as much to Caddy, and she had to agree with him.

"It will be even better when we wake up the rest. That's going to take some time and work, but we will get there."

Caddy yawned; the heat was making her sleepy.

"How long do you think it will take you?"

"Oh, decades probably. Maybe hundreds of years. I don't know." Neptune moved next to her and stroked her back like he would a favourite cat. "But with you here, it won't matter how long it takes."

"DECADES! CENTURIES!" Caddy bolted upright and stared at him. "I'm not staying here for centuries! I'm not staying here for a week! I'm due back in two days!"

Neptune smiled and patted her butt where the sexy blue streaks faded into the green. He liked her butt.

"Love, there could be hundreds of thousands of merfolk sleeping in the deep. You haven't been to the really deep parts yet because you're not ready. But you will be. We haven't even been to the cold waters or the waters on the other side of the world. I'm the Realm Lord of all the oceans and seas, not just the one around your little island! "

He didn't stop, not realising he was digging a hole.

"Your singing will wake them up much faster than we could without you. And you're so clever with humans. You'll be very useful. You're a treasure! And you're beautiful now!"

She shook her head. How could he even imagine such a thing?

"I am going back to Lowestoft! I can't stay here. What about the elves?"

This was a complication. Neptune never thought she would object to staying on, not now that she was a gorgeous mermaid. How could she object? Did he have to explain the obvious?

"Love, this is your home. Not on land with humans. Not with the elves."

He was not happy with the blank expression on her face. Or was it horror?

"Look at you! Can't you see it? You are in your best form, the way you are supposed to be. You are healthy, happy, and beautiful. You are in the *place* where you are supposed to be, which is with me. Don't you feel it? Don't you know it in your bones? You love me, I know you do."

You love me, he said. He didn't say he loved her. All Caddy could do was stare at him, at the ego of him.

And then he made his biggest mistake. It was years before he understood, but this was it –

"You are quite good enough to be a worthy consort for me. When you bond you'll be very happy with me."

Good enough.

Adequate to requirements.

Number two.

"No," she said.

Not "Maybe." Not "But." No equivocation or bargaining. Just "No."

Emphatically no.

Neptune turned, shocked.

"What do you mean – no?" he growled. The merfolk stopped what they were doing and fell silent. Even the children felt the change and they sped to their mothers.

"I'm not staying here. I have to go back to land and to my people. You know that. I said one week. I never promised to be here for decades or forever."

Caddy looked into Neptune's eyes.

"Would you come to live with me for decades, on land, with my elves? Would you help me wake them up?"

"Don't be an idiot, Caddy. I won't go on land to wake up fekkin' elves and leave my people to rot at the bottom of the sea. I have work here."

Sadness, anger, frustration, and then realisation all passed over Neptune's face in the space of a second, and without another word he flopped back into the ocean and swam away. Caddy didn't follow. The merfolk did and in the space of a minute she was alone on the beach, lying back on the sand. And all that was left to do was to stare at the sky.

Neptune left and he didn't come back. Caddy could have chased him down, but she didn't.

Neptune had convinced her to change her body to suit himself and he simply assumed that by becoming a mermaid she was now one of *his* mermaids. Sure, being a mermaid was fun and they all thought she was beautiful and sexy. She saw the looks the mermen shot her when Neptune's back was turned. Sure, she could dive to the bottom of the sea now and there were new wonders just waiting to be explored. And yes, now that she had the correct Slot A to his Tab B, she could have great merfolk sex with Neptune whenever and wherever she wanted.

And, in his own fishy way, he loved her. She knew that. And she loved him.

But she didn't love him enough to be content with being "good enough" for him.

She didn't love him enough to be one in a line of concubines, whatever title he gave her.

She didn't love him enough to give up who she was.

She didn't love him enough to give up her elves.

She didn't love him enough to let the world stay unbalanced.

Being a mermaid was fun, but it was just surface decoration. It was cosplay. It wasn't who she was. Lord Cadence Miller Aeldor wasn't a mermaid.

She lay on her back and looked at the clouds and thought wouldn't it be nice to have legs again – and there was a burst of heat, a tearing and a flash of excruciating pain. She looked down and she had legs.

It felt right. It was who she was and she was very happy with that.

Caddy walked to the cabana and rooted around for her wetsuit, at the same time calling for Ser. It took a few minutes, but he popped in and smiled at her.

"What do you need, Lord Cadence?"

She pointed to the suitcase with the beach towels in it and said, "I need to get this and myself back to Lowestoft. Please port me there."

He didn't look happy. "Lord Neptune –"

"Lord Neptune gave me his word I could go back at any time, and you would take me. You know that. I want to go. Now."

She took a bit of pity on him.

"He knows."

Ser nodded, called a mate to take the suitcase, and within seconds they were gone. He ported her to deep water where he then made another portal under the water. With her mermaid experience gained in the last week she had no problems swimming through the portal by herself and with a shock she was in the ice cold murky English Channel. When she surfaced she could see Lowestoft's South Beach just out of reach. Ser and his friend carried her and the bag close to the shore where she thanked them and swam the last twenty yards by herself, towing the floating bag. When she turned to wave goodbye there was no one to wave to. They were gone.

When a bedraggled, soaking wet, and painfully thin Caddy walked into the back office, no one was expecting her. She wasn't due back for at least a day and the phone, which she had forgotten, and the other bag were still pinging faithfully from the cabana.

She grinned and waved to the elves working the
cubicle pit, and they mobbed her, screaming and laughing
and crying, and she hugged them back, jumping up and
down and laughing. No one cared that she was a sandy,
soaking, seaweedy mess. In the chaotic joy Caddy stepped
back and fell over the suitcase which burst open throwing
bags of what she thought were hermetically sealed stinky
beach towels onto the office floor.

Not sealed enough, it turned out, because suddenly
the place was a riot of reeling drunken women calling
lustily for their men. Then came the loud cries from men
popping in from the middle of whatever they were doing to
rescue them and port them home to tend to their needs
before someone else did.

Norma ran in wearing a gas mask and gave Caddy a
big hug. Caddy couldn't understand a word she was saying
through the mask, so she just pointed behind her, said
"Oops! Sorry about that!" and asked if someone could port
her home. She needed a shower.

She took a long shower and flopped on her lumpy
bed and slept. She dreamed of Ricky.

Caddy, 1948

It was 1948, and Caddy was 23. She worked on the transistor line of Pye's Television Factory in Lowestoft. The managers hired women to do the fiddly work because they had nimble fingers and were careful and accurate. They were also paid half of what a man was paid. Even if men couldn't do the job and women did it better they were still paid half because that was the natural order of things. A few radical suffragette types complained, but the vast majority of the Pye Girls were just happy to feed their children. Many were sole breadwinners and after the war men were thin on the ground in Lowestoft.

She lived on the top floor of a purpose built flat on London Road South where she had a nice roommate who, like Caddy, was single and she paid half the rent and expenses. They got along fine. Her name was Clara.

Clara was desperate to get married and not just to anyone but to an American. Even years after the war, England was still flooded with Americans and there were several small air bases dotted around Norfolk and Suffolk. According to Clara, each tiny airfield held a potential husband. Her only goal in life was to go to America and live in a nice ranch house in suburbia and drive a flash car to the shops just like what she saw in the cinema. Clara's desperation wasn't really to snag a husband; her consuming desire was to live in a Hollywood B movie.

To that end Clara haunted the public ballrooms where the American GIs went on their nights off to dance and drink, and if they got lucky, screw a sweet English Rose. Clara was smart enough not to get one of *those* reputations, and she only went to the nicer dance halls, and she always went with a pack of girlfriends to provide protection and cover if she needed it.

Caddy never went with her. For one thing, she didn't dance. Not a bit. For another, she wasn't much of a drinker and didn't find it entertaining to watch other people get stupid. And thirdly, she was plain. Not being a looker, especially if she was in a pack of prettier girls, she didn't have men chatting her up in a noisy club. To the young men Caddy was work, and there were easier, prettier, more entertaining girls to woo. The GIs had their choice of flocks of eager fun-loving dance partners, each prettier than the last and all more worthy of spending their pay packets on than a plain shy wallflower.

So what was the point of getting dressed up to buy your own drinks, watch other people have a good time and be ignored? A Saturday night at home with a good book or playing her guitar was so much more fun.

But today desperate times called for desperate measures, and Clara was desperate. All of her usual dance mates had cancelled and for some of the stupidest reasons. Getting married *next* week was not a reason to not go out dancing *this* week. Twisting your ankle was not a reason to stay home. And those were just two of the better excuses. The others were worse.

She had a fine fish on the line, an American Air
Force sergeant (!) out of Lakenheath. Never married.
Tallish, good looking, built like a rugby player, with a fine
head of hair and a good dancer, and who, bless, seemed to
have the hots for her. She knew if she didn't go out and
meet him at the Pally in Norwich he'd just find some other
girl to spend his Saturday and his money on and Clara
might lose him forever. She was *not* going to let that
happen! So to keep her good girl reputation intact she
needed to find another good girl to go with her, and that girl
was going to be Sad Sack Caddy. She was all that was left.
And Robert wouldn't flirt with her. No one ever did.

"C'mon, Caddy, it'll be fun!"

Clara begged – absolutely begged – Caddy to put a
nice dress on, do something with her hair, and come to the
Pally with her so she could spend some time with her new
prospect.

Caddy sighed and went along. It was just a Saturday
night, and she would give that up for Clara because she
knew how much it meant to her. Clara said she would pay
for the train and that Robert would buy her a drink, so all
Caddy had to do was sit and be pleasant and not get in the
way of True Love. Just in case she sat alone Caddy stuck a
crossword puzzle in her purse.

The Pally was ear-splittingly noisy and jam-packed with airmen, GIs, pretty girls, and surly demobbed local lads who didn't have the money the Americans had. There was a bar in the front, a bandstand in the back, a huge dance floor in the middle, and tables arranged around the perimeter and more chairs along the walls. Fogging everything was a thick haze of cigarette smoke that stung Caddy's eyes and made her sneeze.

Robert roped in a barracks rat to keep whoever Clara had hauled in with her occupied. If everything went the way he wanted they could split off and have a little feel-good session in the back of his car in the parking lot. He made sure he parked in a nice dark corner.

Caddy and Clara walked in, and after pushing their way through the crowd (Clara doing the pushing; she was determined) they found Robert and his Air Force friend sitting at a tiny table. They already had pints on the table waiting for the girls, and Caddy could see a couple of empty glasses, so someone had been drinking to kill time. Robert introduced his barracks mate, Ricky, and Clara introduced her flatmate, Caddy, and they promptly disappeared in the scrum of the dancefloor leaving Caddy and Ricky to stare at each other and pretend they were having a good time.

Ricky looked like he was all of fourteen. Shy, slender, sandy-haired, and the same height as Caddy, which meant that for a man he was a couple of inches under average. He was from Texas. He thought Caddy was beautiful.

Caddy, for her part, was happy that Ricky was not a total arse. Her flatmate tended to attract jerks and she wasn't impressed with Clara's new Robert. There was something mean in those glittering eyes and when she saw him walk Clara to the dance floor his rolling gait reminded her of her father.

"D-do you want to dance?" Ricky had a slight stutter when he was nervous, and Caddy made him nervous.

"No, thank you. I don't dance. Never learned." Caddy smiled brightly, sure he would be relieved. And she was right; he was. He didn't want to dance with her either.

Ricky took a small sip of his beer and shifted in his chair. He didn't have a clue what to say to this red-haired girl with the bright green eyes.

She was wearing a pretty yellow dress with a wide boat neck that dipped just below her collar bones. It was a modest dress, but those collar bones, that neck –

Ricky didn't know if he could handle looking at much more than that.

"Do you know Babe Ruth's real name?"

Ricky started. He was staring at Caddy's neck. "George Herman Ruth."

"Thank you!" And Caddy pulled *The Times* Sunday crossword out of her handbag along with a pen and wrote in Herman. Forty-Seven across. Ricky looked over and moved his chair so he was next to her and not across the table, took a big swig of beer, and then gave her the answer to 12 down. And that's what they did all evening. The rest of the world danced around them, but Ricky and Caddy sat so close their heads touched, and they worked on *The Times* crossword puzzle.

They almost finished it, too.

Caddy

Caddy sat in her office, working *The Times* crossword puzzle, a cup of tea steaming next to her. The hidden speakers softly played some old dance music from one of her playlists.

Ellen shut the door behind her and sat down. She brought in her own cup of tea and took a sip.

"So, what happened?"

Caddy looked up and smiled.

"You don't beat around the bush do you?"

"No point in it, Caddy."

Caddy put down her pen and cradled her tea with both hands.

"It didn't work out. It won't ever work out. He's sea and I'm land. Together we made mud." Caddy paused. Ellen didn't say anything.

"He expected me to do all of the adjusting and he thought he was the one making all the concessions. He wanted me to go live with him, wake up his merfolk, and be a good PA for Neptune, Ltd. And he thought the occasional good bonk would be enough to tempt me to agree."

Ellen winced and nodded. She expected something like that.

"I'm sorry, Caddy."

Caddy shrugged. "It wasn't all bad, you know. I had some really good times with Neptune, and I'm not talking about the sex. I learned a few things about myself, and Ellen, I'm well over a hundred so it's not often I learn something new about myself. I learned to…" Her voice faded away.

"Anyway, it's over, and he won't be back." She took a sip of tea. "And if he did come looking for me – and he won't – I wouldn't take him back. Not as a lover. I don't think he hates me, and I don't hate him, but –"

Caddy sighed.

"Mutual disappointment I guess."

"Tell the ladies not to waste the beach towels. I don't have any other boyfriends in sight and there aren't any other lords out there. My last dry spell lasted thirty years."

Ellen smiled weakly.

"I'm sorry Caddy. I love you. We all love you."

"I know you do, dear. I love you, too. That's why I'm not dancing topless on a tropical beach with mermaids right now."

She looked in her teacup.

"Love isn't what you say, Ellen, it's what you do."

Ellen left and shut the door softly behind her. And Caddy returned to her crossword puzzle.

Ricky, 1949

Ricky pursued Caddy as relentlessly as Clara pursued Robert, and they both won their prize. But Ricky would have said his prize was the only one worth winning.

Caddy didn't go to the dance halls, so on Sundays Ricky took the train down to Lowestoft which suited him much better anyway. During good weather he took her on long walks on the Prom or on a picnic. During bad weather they went to the cinema.

He never met her parents and didn't ask why. Once she saw one of her brothers in the cinema and pointed him out to Ricky, but she didn't go to him, and, if the brother saw his sister and her boyfriend in the US Air Force uniform, he didn't acknowledge them.

Ricky was nineteen when he met Caddy. He was barely twenty when he asked her to marry him. She said no. Besides, the Air Force wouldn't give him permission to marry until he was a sergeant.

The girls at Pye's knew all about US Air Force regulations regarding marriage to foreign nationals because Clara wasn't the only one on the hunt. The war had knocked England back hard and Lowestoft was a tough town to be poor in. But if you married an airman Uncle Sam gave you a golden ticket to America – The Land of the Free and The Home of Indoor Plumbing.

Ricky was an intelligence analyst and at his rank of senior airman he was not much more than a file clerk; there were a million of them, and after the war promotions were rare, so to make rank he decided to go into an area where there were more openings. When he found out that there was a big demand for Russian linguists he simply learned Russian.

Everyone who knew Ricky would tell you he was a genius. He never forgot anything if he put his formidable mind to it *and* if he considered it worth remembering. But more than simply memorising data, he could see relationships, patterns, cause and effect, and predict outcomes. He could analyse. He couldn't tell you Caddy's birthday or recall the colour of Lizzie's eyes, but to his dying day he could decline Russian verbs or go deep into the technical details of the Sukhoi Su-24's integrated digital navigation and attack system and he could tell you why both were important.

Learning Russian took him six months. He wasn't proficient, but he was good enough to pass a test and that earned him another stripe. It also meant he would be transferred to Germany – to Berlin – and if Caddy was to go with him they must be married. This time she didn't say no. She said she would think about it.

He called her every Wednesday at six just to see what she was doing and to hear her voice. Rain or shine, she walked to the corner to a red BT phone booth and waited for him to call, and they would chat for about ten minutes to plan what to do on Sunday.

One Wednesday she told him Clara was moving out. Her roommate was marrying Robert. She was also pregnant. Then Caddy asked Ricky if he knew what a condom was. He thought this was going to be a joke at Clara's expense, so he laughed and said yes, Robert was the one who needed to learn about birth control. And Caddy laughed and said, "Bring a box with you on Sunday and we'll see if you can do better than Robert." And she hung up.

Early on, Caddy told Ricky about her aborted first marriage to a bigamist and that she wasn't a virgin, because if that was going to be a deal breaker, early was the time to get it out in the open. He said it didn't matter at all; he had his own past girlfriends and if she was okay with his past then he was okay with hers. She was telling the truth, but Ricky lied. There were no previous girlfriends.

In the end it didn't matter at all. She was new to him, and he was new to her, and they both were very happy with every wonderful new discovery.

Caddy

If Ellen and Norma were worried about Caddy, they were the only ones. The men didn't see any difference in her at all. The lord was cheerful, she cracked jokes, she was interested in every aspect of elf life, but she never interfered with it. The shop was the same; she had run it for decades, but now a company of elves did, and it was doing great. They didn't need her advice.

Every morning she was up at dawn, ate breakfast at eight, went to the shop at 9:30, went back home at 4:00, had dinner at 6:00, and was in bed by 10:00. She practised her abilities and her music for hours every day.

Once a week Caddy would go and play in an outlying village and wake up more elves. She never got tired of doing that, and it was always the highlight of her week.

Life was settling into a comfortable routine.

The more comfortable and routine it got, the more Ellen and Norma fretted.

Tony, Vernon, and Norma

After work, Tony, Vernon, and Norma sat in "their" booth at the pub and Norma brooded.

"She is playing that damn cello all the time now. All. The. Time."

"What's wrong with the cello? I like cello music." Vernon sat back and stroked his beard. "Besides, she practises on everything."

Norma glared. How could Vernon be so dense?

"Guitar good. Violin neutral. Cello bad." Norma took an impressive swig of her beer. "She's depressed. If she were playing the cello once every few weeks I'd say it was just practise, but it's *all* the damn time. "

"Maybe breaking up with Neptune was harder on her than we thought. I've noticed that she's plateaued on her health. She was getting much healthier when she was with Neptune. Even after he left, she was getting better. But since she came back? I don't know. I thought I saw a new age spot on her hand the other day."

"Yep, she's definitely plateaued. She looked about human fifty when she went off to that damned island, but I would add five years to that now." Norma looked around the pub. It was getting busier and noisier. Oh, well, they'd leave soon anyway.

"But I don't think it's Neptune. I really do think she is getting over that disaster. I think it's deeper."

"What do you mean?"

"Tony, how did you feel when you thought you were the only elf alive?" Norma looked at her phone. The unanswered messages were piling up. "How do you think she feels to be the only female lord alive and the only male lord has turned out to be a 'disappointment' and has now disappeared, probably for good?"

"Wow. You're just a ray of sunshine, Norma. I thought she was doing all right, but now I'm going to worry about her for the rest of the night."

Norma shrugged. Vernon had a bonded wife to
sleep next to. Neither she nor Tony nor Caddy did.
Because of Caddy, she and Tony might find someone out
there. There was always that hope, but Caddy was the last
white rhino aging away in the zoo. Pampered and loved
and utterly alone.

"I'm heading home. There's nothing we can do but
let nature take its course. This world is thin on lords, but if
one rose out of the sea before, maybe one will fall out of
the sky next time. Who knows. We just have to do our best
to keep her happy and healthy. Good night!"

And Norma popped out, leaving the two men to
brood in their beer.

Caddy

The dream was so clear. So real. Caddy knew it was
a dream, but do you smell things in dreams? Stale cigarette
smoke and musty maps and that indefinable mix of man
sweat and the coarse lye soap the charwoman used to scrub
the floors? Can you feel the texture of the worn leather seat
of the office chair in a dream?

Caddy dreamed she was sitting in a windowless office in the basement of an anonymous office building in the Allied Sector of Berlin. It was Ricky's old office. She had been in it only once before because dependents weren't allowed in classified areas, but one afternoon it had been scrubbed of anything sensitive, and on a Wives' Day she was invited in for coffee and cookies and she was permitted to see where her husband spent his days. The general's wife thought it would improve morale.

But in her dream no one was there just her and Ricky. The rows of desks were empty and this time the walls weren't sanitised; they were covered in maps. Map cases lined every available wall space, and Caddy knew there were back storage rooms of nothing but more maps.

Ricky was at his desk, looking at a map and mumbling to himself. Caddy knew this was a dream because the room was 1953 Berlin, but this was 2001 Ricky. He was wearing the same clothes he wore on his last trip to Asda.

He looked up and smiled, a cigarette dangling from his mouth. He had given up smoking in '73 when he caught the boys playing with a pack of his cigs, but obviously had taken it up again.

"Hi, Caddy. Long time, no see."

"Hiya, Ricky. You're looking good. Smoking again, I see."

Now he grinned. He knew she didn't like him smoking. "It doesn't matter any more, Caddy. You know that. What's it going to do, kill me?" He looked back at the map.

"Can't stay long, honey; lots to do. Lines on maps. They're moving."

Lines on maps. Ricky was a master strategist. He didn't play chess because it was too easy. He played the armies of the world and it was in post-war Berlin where he learned his craft and where the Air Force learned about Ricky. Before computers it was all on paper. Little slips of paper with coded notes that meant nothing to anyone but Ricky. Notes that said this Russian platoon didn't have lunch yesterday. That a minor Polish unit was moving to the Estonian border. These jets were down for maintenance. Constant bits of random information were fed into the gristmill that was Ricky's brain, and he would plot them on a map, think about what it meant and tell his officers what was going to happen.

Because a little man sat in a basement and looked at lines on maps, reports could be fed up to colonels who put their own names on cover sheets and fed the information to generals who knew who really did the work because they had been colonels themselves once. The reports were sent on to presidents and prime ministers, and every western government knew what was going to happen. So Balance was maintained. No nukes went flying, no massive armies moved, and no panicked reactions from the West to provocations and emergencies. Oh, there were wars; decision makers didn't always pay attention to what they were told, so Korea, Vietnam, and the Middle East flared up. But in the context of history the wars were small, friction was minor, and the world had a long long period of relative peace.

Ricky was always right. For that they put up with his irritating quirks and found good paying jobs with bland titles where he could sit and look at maps. Every couple of years someone in human resources or a captain on an efficiency drive would come in and try to fire the odd little man who didn't seem to have any purpose other than to look at lines on maps, and then some general would jump on them with both feet and tell them to GTFO. And Ricky would go back to his desk, usually with a pay rise, and spend his mornings looking at maps. Later in life he gave classes to officers about strategy and tactics.

"Here. This is where they'll breach if you don't get your ass in gear." He looked at Caddy, and now he wasn't smiling. "You gotta stop thinking about me, hon. You're doing a good job. Keep it up."

Tears started flowing down Caddy's cheeks.

"I miss you, Ricky. I didn't even get to say goodbye."

He grimaced and had to look back down at his map. Ricky hated seeing Caddy cry. Oh, he got mad at her, furious even. Their marriage had its desperate low points, and there were times when he wondered if they could hang on, but he could never walk out the door because if he did she'd cry.

"It was my time, hon. It was a good way to go, you know that. But you gotta turn off the waterworks, babe. Stop moping about the past. You gotta move forward. It's all up to you now.'

"What's up to me, Ricky?"

He looked up, surprised she had to ask.

"Lines on maps, babe. Lines on maps."

Caddy

Morning dawned, bright and clear; today was going to be one of those rare glorious late August days when the normally grey East of England seaside would rival any tropical strand.

It was going to be a scorcher and the beach would soon be chock-a-block with determined Brits on beach blankets complaining about the heat, drinking hot tea, and flirting with skin cancer.

Today Caddy decided to walk to the office. It would be a sin to port when she could breathe in the sea air and see the North Sea glisten a rare blue. Well, a greyish blue. There were already sailboats playing close to shore, and far out, well past the shoals and where the earth curved away from the sky, Caddy could see the faint grey outlines of cargo tankers as they wound their way through the busiest shipping channel in the world. Outside of Lowestoft the world was moving.

Seagulls screamed and swooped and fearlessly waddled around the Prom looking for the odd dropped chip. She looked for Jack, but he was nowhere to be seen; and on the beach she didn't see any merfolk. And, of course, no Neptune.

She was alone but not alone. All around were elves. Oh, she didn't see a one, but they were there; she knew it. She could feel them.

And people. Humans were everywhere. Messy, loud, frustrating, comical, endearing humans poured from the homes on the estates and terraces and flooded to the beach. In the crowd was the occasional orc, ready to stir up a bit of chaos and make life interesting. The humans didn't know the orcs were orcs, but then – neither did the orcs. Not yet. But Caddy knew that enlightenment was coming. It had to now that elves were back. Balance will be served.

The prom was getting crowded. Lowestoft families, some happy, some already cross, herded their excited children ahead and carried much-too-much brightly coloured crap down the cliff to the sands in search of the perfect spot to play and relax and maybe to dream.

Pretty girls, self-conscious and wearing too little, strutted down the prom in giggling flocks followed by young men lured by hope and the girls' undefinable perfume floating in the breeze.

Caddy stood at the top of the cliff and looked to the east and, like Neptune not so long ago, was well-pleased with the happy and contented scene spreading out below her. It was as it should be.

More and more chattering, happy people came to the beach, and they brushed by her, not paying the least attention to the middle-aged lady in the straw hat, striped Breton top, and shorts, looking at the sea and smiling to herself. She looked exactly like everyone's middle-class, middle-aged, middle-England neighbour – the one who plants pansies in her garden and waves when you walk by. She was exactly like a hundred nans down on the beach slathering sunscreen on their grandkids. She was ubiquitous yet invisible.

Caddy took another deep breath and beamed at nothing in particular. Then Lord Cadence Aeldor of Lowestoft, Suffolk County, wife, mother, lover, retired teacher, business owner, musician, and Queen of the Fairies, turned and walked to her office.

She had work to do.

End of Book 1

Book 2

I Do Wander Everywhere

and more books in this series are available for
download on
Amazon Kindle or
The Rum Lot Publishing

www.rumlot.com

Donate to the Excelsior Trust

If you enjoyed this book (and we hope you did!), please consider a small donation to The Excelsior Trust, a registered charity that is dedicated to preserving heritage fishing boats, in particular The Excelsior, LT 472.   As part of the trust's mission to preserve Britain's maritime heritage they also subsidise unique training and sailing experiences for young people.

https://www.theexcelsiortrust.co.uk/

https://www.theexcelsiortrust.co.uk/donate

Registered Charity Number 285899

www.ingramcontent.com/pod-product-compliance
Lightning Source LLC
Chambersburg PA
CBHW020324180626
46812CB00001B/36